I0623963

NUTS

THE ACE'S WILD SERIES

SE JAKES

NUTS

Jagger's the son of a bookmaker and fixer. Now, he's the owner of an exclusive, underground club...he's also been put in charge of the family business.

Preston's the son of a wealthy, powerful, blue-blood Boston family...or he was, until he was disowned for choosing his friendship with Jagger over his family. Ten years later, he's a Special Forces Operator—and he's still best friends with Jagger.

But things are about to change, for both men. Because after a long year of no contact, Preston's coming home to Jagger for the first time since they shared a surprising kiss.

One night, one poker game, and one hand finds Jagger lucky—and skilled enough—to win a chance to fix things with Preston. But what's at stake is far more than their friendship—it's everything...and both men are all in to fight for what's theirs.

FOREWORD

Ace's Wild is a multi-author series of books that take place in the same fictional town. Each story can be read in any order. The connecting element in the Ace's Wild series is an adult store owned by Ace and Wilder. The main characters from each book will make at least one visit to Ace's Wild, where they'll buy a toy to use in their story! The only characters who cross over to each book are Ace and Wilder. And with various heat and kink levels, there's sure to be something for everyone!

Thanks for giving the series a chance! We hope you enjoy the books!

Christina Lee, Riley Hart, SE Jakes, Alice Winters, Devon McCormack, Max Walker, Annabella Michaels, Neve Wilder, Jaclyn Quinn, Morningstar Ashley, Davidson King, NR Walker, Luna David, & Lane Hayes.

Nuts:

The best possible poker hand one can have at any given moment.

PROLOGUE

Jagger

Then.

BASTARD SON OF A SINNER.

Family of sinners.

In bed with the devil.

This bastard son of a sinner was too well respected—feared, even —for anyone to say it to his face. Not without enticing a beating. He wasn't a violent kid by nature, but he'd learned early on that he had a family reputation to uphold, that the streets were his as long as he took control of them. Of himself. His father and uncles had stepped in to train him to fight early—both with boxing rules and dirty street fighting.

So Jagger ignored what he heard murmured today—he'd heard all of it and more, and well before his mom's death. Heard it, discarded it, because he knew Maggie King better than anyone else outside his family.

He knew the truth.

He still felt hollow as fuck as he walked like a zombie through the halls of his Boston high school, on the first day of his junior year. He should've cut, because today was all about reuniting with friends, bragging about summer vacation, and reestablishing yourself as the shit.

He didn't have to reestablish shit. He needed to mourn his mother. But she'd made him promise that he wouldn't do that, and hers were the orders he'd always followed, without question.

Now, over the usual, expected rumblings from behind his back, he heard others too, and this time, they weren't about him. They filtered into his consciousness like a warning, a skitter of awareness up his spine that something happened, a shift in his usual universe.

Pretty boy thinks he's better than us.

Rich kid slumming.

Ruin that pretty face.

But this time, they definitely weren't about him. Jagger was never a pretty boy, but the new kid most definitely was. A blond, movie-star-looking guy walking the halls of this less-than-stellar public school would get a lot of attention, both good and bad, and today it was definitely more on the bad side.

He was also holding himself stiffly—pride, maybe, for someone who didn't look closely, and Jagger was relatively certain pretty boy was trying not to let everyone know he'd taken a bad beating recently. He also looked pissed off at the universe.

Jagger would only find out later that Preston had been kicked out of several private schools already, that sending him here, to one of Boston's toughest public high schools, was a punishment his parents had thrust on him. But even then, seeing him for the first time, Jagger was instantly aware of how pretty boy held himself straight and tall, completely aware of his surroundings.

He doesn't belong here.

But inexplicably, somehow pretty boy did belong there, seemed far more of Jagger's world, even with his movie-star good looks and preppy clothes.

Jagger saw the other signs of the gathering perfect storm. The dismissal bell. The emptying halls. The boys who were no doubt lying in wait just outside school grounds, waiting to follow through on their threats to ruin the rich kid's face, and that's what had Jagger shaking off his haze of mourning.

If nothing else, Jagger's bad reputation could do pretty boy some good. And so Jagger trailed just behind him...until he got to the gates of the parking lot, where a group of at least ten boys waited.

To his credit, he just kept walking.

"Hey, pretty boy—"

"Name's Preston," pretty boy said clearly. Unafraid.

"Yeah, we know. Preston VanValen," Trumble mimicked in a high voice, and Jagger went still. Because what were the goddamned chances he would be exactly where he needed to be?

He took a deep breath and accepted his fate by walking up next to Preston. He'd have done it anyway, last name be damned. With that, Trumble, who hated Jagger almost as much as he feared him, narrowed his eyes and waited for Jagger's next move. Which was putting a hand on his shoulder for the briefest of seconds. "Let's go, Preston."

"Beauty and the fucking beast," Trumble muttered.

Jagger laughed and turned to Preston. "Let's go, beauty." He jerked his chin for Preston to follow, saw his jaw clench and the slight hesitation before he did what Jagger had asked.

"Sure you want to throw your protection his way, Jagger?" Trumble called from behind them.

Jagger just kept walking, Preston by his side. By the time they'd gotten to the end of the block, the angry group of boys had dissipated.

That's when Preston turned on him, furious. "You just made shit worse for me. I'm not your pet."

Jagger ignored the jabs. "How're you getting home?"

Preston frowned. "Do you not understand English?" he demanded, and Jagger simply waited. "I'm walking. Not that it matters to you."

"How far?"

Preston sighed. "Five miles. Maybe more. I'll clock it for you and report back in the morning."

"It'll take you hours." *And leave you vulnerable.*

"It's good practice."

Jagger didn't ask for what. Instead, he stayed beside Preston for the long, laborious walk home. Preston's ribs were most definitely broken.

"This is me," Preston said finally, pointing to the large gate that was no doubt meant to keep people out. Jagger saw it as more of a way for Preston to be forced to stay locked in. "Look, take back your protection, or whatever the hell you're doing. Don't get involved."

"I already am."

"Why?"

"I think we should be friends."

Preston snorted. "What do you want from me? Protection money? I've got none."

The irony of him saying that while standing outside of a mansion wasn't lost on Jagger. It didn't matter though—Jagger didn't want Preston's money. "I didn't walk you here for money, okay?"

"Right. Just out of the goodness of your heart."

"Yeah. I guess it was bound to happen someday."

"I heard them talking about you," Preston told him. "Is it true your mom just died?"

"Yeah, it is."

"I'm sorry."

There was something so sincere about the way Preston said those words that made Jagger's insides twist and Maggie's words ring in his ears.

You'll know when you're in the right place, Jagger. Trust in that. Trust that you'll find the right people and when you do, keep them in your life no matter what. "We're going to be friends," he told Preston stubbornly.

Preston shook his head. "I can't have friends. My family ruins things."

"My family fixes them," Jagger assured him.

"No one can fix this."

"You've never met anyone like me."

From anyone else, it would've sounded like boasting, but Jagger was so goddamned sincere. And still, Preston rolled his eyes and muttered, "Asshole with an ego."

"And it only took you an hour to figure that out."

Preston
Then.

For the first several years Preston and Jagger had been friends, Preston hadn't known what the King family did for a living beyond own the bar. There were always rumors, but growing up in South Boston, it didn't matter what side of the tracks you were from—the mob was always a shadow.

By the time Preston turned seventeen, he'd learned that Jagger's family ran book—sports betting and the like. He wasn't allowed to know the full extent of it or why gambling could be illegal, and he didn't want to.

Jagger hadn't wanted him to know either.

"But you're learning it," Preston had asked, lying on Jagger's bed while Jagger paged through the mysterious book he always had with him these days.

"It's more than learning it," he'd explained. "It's like it's always been there. I grew up with it. I can't not know it."

"Numbers."

He nodded. Jagger had always been freaky good with numbers. Apparently that and a kind of gambling sixth sense ran in their family.

Thankfully, addiction didn't. Maybe because they were surrounded by it with the people they served.

They hadn't created them, but Preston knew the whole family absorbed the guilt of it.

The addicts weren't the ones who funded the business. They were small potatoes, and more than once, he'd watched Jagger's dad forgive a debt so a family wouldn't go hungry.

Preston had never seen his parents help anyone but themselves. After meeting Jagger, it hadn't taken Preston long to realize that his own family's business dealings weren't one hundred percent on the up-and-up—not even close—but in their circles, it was considered business.

The neighborhood Jagger lived in was rough and oh so different than Preston's. He much preferred Jagger's world. No one sugarcoated anything. For the most part, the only people who got hurt were those who played and then didn't pay. The Kings didn't deal with small-time folks. No, they repped much bigger game, Irish mob territory, and they kept their noses clean.

It didn't stop the police from haunting their doorsteps though, and Jagger—and Preston too—got used to seeing the uniformed officers.

By the time Preston was seventeen, he was practically living full-time with the Kings. They sheltered him from the business, but Preston was always watching out for Jagger, as if he knew his friend could face trouble at any moment.

Usually, it was just some punks trying to take on a King. Jagger could more than take care of himself, but Preston protected his best friend as fiercely as Jagger protected him from the shit his family tried to pull. And Preston was big and strong enough, and had enough of Jagger's friends usually surrounding him.

Today, though, he didn't have that cushion. He wouldn't have it again later that night, when it was especially important, and none of it was his fault or Jagger's.

No, the police were actively working to dismantle the last of the old guard Boston mob, which was a losing proposition, no matter how you looked at it. Preston wondered why they didn't go after the gangs or the motorcycle clubs who worked with the mob rather than hitting up local businessmen with only the most tenuous—and unproven—connections to organized crime.

Today, Preston was that most tenuous connection, and when the two undercover officers grabbed him on the walk back to Jagger's house and stuffed him into the back of the police car, Preston got an early start in interrogation techniques.

Jagger was home sick that day. The men who'd grabbed him had to know that. Had to have been watching. Maybe they'd even arranged for his extra-long detention session, which let him out too late for anyone to see him get yanked into the police car.

First, the police had questioned him, picked him up, and kept him in a room without food or water or a bathroom break. By the time they'd let him out, his phone battery was dead and it was dark out.

The police had definitely made a few calls to let people know his location and that he'd be alone.

He made it three blocks from the station when he heard the usual catcalls start.

"Hey, pretty boy."

"There's Jagger's pet, off his leash."

"Well now, here's a sight you don't see often—Preston VanValen without his backup." Trumble stepped out in front of him.

"Fuck off, Trumble." Preston waved him off. Too many of these guys were wannabe gangsters, their fathers low-level mob guys who drank and fucked too much to be of any real use to anyone. Their kids threatened to grow up in their exact image.

Tonight, there were six of them and one of him, and Preston knew that the police had done this, left him vulnerable to teach him a lesson.

This will teach him a lesson, Priscilla. His father's words biting into his ear after he'd endured the last beating he'd ever taken from the man. Even with his father threatening to call the police on Preston if he didn't stand down, Preston refused to let himself get hit again.

In the aftermath of taking a severe beating, but still bearing the satisfaction of having crushed Trumble's nose to fucking bits, Preston managed to somehow make it to the Kings'. He half crawled into the alley, well aware that of what would've happened if the car hadn't come by and scared away Trumble and his friends.

Now, he knocked on the kitchen door as loud as he could but passed out before anyone came to get him. It was only when one of the cooks came out for a cigarette break and hit Preston's body with the door that he'd been discovered, brought inside, taken upstairs.

"It might scar" was all he remembered the doctor saying.

"Doesn't matter," Preston had mumbled.

When he woke, it was two days later. Jagger was by his side and refused to leave. Later, Preston heard through the grapevine that what happened to him didn't go unavenged, on any front.

Three weeks later, he'd be disinherited and disowned, taken in by Jagger's family...and on a bus to basic training.

CHAPTER ONE

Jagger

Now.

JAGGER KING almost ignored his ringing phone, but a nagging sense of duty forced him to excuse himself from the man who'd been flirting with him all night to check. He walked away from his recent conquest completely when he saw Preston's number on the screen.

Preston. After three hundred and seventy-nine days of utter, heart-breaking silence, Preston was finally calling.

His departure hadn't been a surprise—he'd been at the start of what he'd hoped was his final year in the Army, and whenever he deployed, he and Jagger would only see each other a handful of times but talk a whole lot more. Except this last time, Jagger was essentially cut off from his best friend, who'd obviously been grateful to run back into the Army and escape what had happened between them.

The silence hadn't been on Jagger's end—he was still texting and leaving messages when Preston's voicemail wasn't full—but he was ultimately talking into the void. His best friend since their junior year of high school had cut him off completely, and all Jagger could do was wait him out.

That stubborn motherfucker had been the one who'd initiated the damned kiss in the first place. "Preston?"

"Hey, Jag. Yeah, it's me." Preston sounded tired. Exhausted, actually, and reluctant. "Sorry to bother you."

"It's never a bother—come on." *You stubborn ass.* "Where are you?" He didn't bother trying to make that last part not sound like a command.

"I'm...back. In North Carolina. I've been staying in a motel for the last week," he finally admitted. "I needed some time to decompress... but it's not working. It's making things worse."

Jagger swallowed hard, hearing the edge of panic in Preston's voice, and tried to keep his tone even. "Where are you, baby? I'll come get you."

"Wait till morning."

"Neither of us is going to get any sleep."

Preston sighed in acknowledgment. "North Ridge."

An hour away. Only a goddamned sixty-minute stretch had separated them for the last week, instead of the half a world Jagger had assumed. "I'm on my way."

"Not alone," Preston instructed suddenly, like he was back in charge of keeping him safe, and Jagger bristled. Mainly because Preston was right.

But that didn't mean Jagger would listen. He pushed down his anger and started his truck, telling Preston, "Please...stay on with me," and making it seem like he was the one who needed the assurance, and hell, it wasn't a lie.

"S'fine. I will." After a pause, Preston continued. "Storm's coming. You're driving into it."

It was why Jagger hadn't taken his Harley—otherwise, he'd force

Preston into the bitch seat to let him know he wasn't getting away anymore. But the rain forced him to be far more subtle, to go slower. "Story of my life, Pres."

Preston gave a sound that was probably supposed to be a laugh but sounded more like he was choking. Whenever he left Jagger's side for any length of time, the man always goddamned forgot how to laugh. "So, what did I interrupt?"

"Nothing much."

"Just your usual Saturday night pickups?"

Jagger wasn't sure what to do with that. Normally, hearing that joking from his straight best friend meant that things were normal between them. But since their kiss—and Preston's subsequent disappearing act—Jagger wasn't sure of anything anymore. "Something like that. No one important."

There was a long pause, as if Preston was absorbing that. "So the club's good?"

"Yeah, it's fine. Always busy." God, this was painful. Jagger pushed the truck faster along the rain-slicked roads, needing to see Preston in person and get rid of this stilted shit. From the moment they'd met, they'd been easy with each other. Joined at the hip, finishing each other's sentences, practically-reading-each-other's-minds easy.

"How's Stuart?"

"He's fine. The same." Stuart was the club manager, and he'd been working for Jagger's family for years in Boston before relocating with Jagger to North Carolina. Jagger knew that Preston didn't like Stuart as much as he appreciated him—Stuart had never been a threat to their friendship, but Stuart's job was to do what was best for Jagger. And Jagger didn't always do what was best for himself, because of Preston. "Dad's good too—enjoying semi-retirement."

"Yeah? I wouldn't think he'd like it much."

Jagger had been surprised too, but after heading the family business of making book for thirty years, Sean Michael King III decided that his oldest son was ready to inherit the good, the bad, and the ugly. The old way of doing things, and the majority of the Boston mob had given way to Armenian gangs, which had Sean mourning the old days. Jagger had to admit that his father was right—there wasn't honor in the game anymore. It was a brute force, zero-sum game. "Dad's actually in Ireland—a three-month tour."

"Back to the motherland?" Preston said it the way Sean always did, and they both laughed. Finally, Preston's real laugh sounded rusty but closer to normal. Jagger's hands loosened slightly from their death grip on the steering wheel.

"This time, he's been threatening to buy land, build a house, and buy a pub," Jagger admitted.

"So much for retirement. Is Seamus running Kings now?"

"Kings" was the original family bar, in the heart of southie Boston. "Seamus is finally growing up. He's been helping to deal with things from that end while I shore up things this way." Jagger had wanted to move the majority of the business dealings, which included the book-making, some real estate, and a few other enterprises that could skate the line of legal to his new club, where there would be less police scrutiny. Less scrutiny from their enemies too, because a lot of the men who normally gave his family trouble wouldn't regularly visit a BDSM club. They'd stick out like sore thumbs among the regular members, who were thoroughly vetted before membership was granted. No one could simply walk in off the street.

Jagger had bought the space three years earlier. It took two of those to get it to where he'd wanted it, and he'd lived above it during that time to oversee construction. Just when everything had fallen into place, his and Preston's friendship had fallen apart.

But not for much longer. "Hey, Pres?"

"Yeah?"

"I'm here." The "for you" hung unspoken between them.

CHAPTER TWO

Preston

PRESTON'S HEART hammered as the big black Suburban pulled into view. "I see you," he told Jagger before cutting the line and walking toward the truck, his bag already on his shoulder. As they'd talked, he'd gone into the motel room and gathered his gear, left his room key on the dresser.

Now, he opened the truck's back door first to put his bag in, but Jagger was already out of the car and hugging him, ignoring the rain.

"Don't ever fucking do that to me again," he murmured fiercely into Preston's ear as his arms tightened around him, and fuck, Jagger was probably the only person Preston could tolerate this kind of touch from right now. He was glad that hadn't changed.

"Sorry" was all he managed before Jagger released him from the hug but still held him at arm's length. "I know what you're doing."

"Making sure everything's in one piece."

"Most everything is."

"You look good, Pres."

"Yeah, you too." Jagger always did in his rough-bearded, messy-haired, strong-featured way. But when he smiled, his entire face broke open, making him look boyish and innocent.

As close to innocent as Jagger could ever look.

Ever since Jagger had grown the beard, Preston had wondered how it would feel against his skin, and now he knew. Fucking amazing—scraping, scratching, leaving his cheeks raw. He'd rubbed his cheeks for days after he'd left Jagger's, and he fought the urge to do it again now, in memory.

"Come on—let's get you home."

Home. Fuck, that was nice to hear.

Being next to Jagger meant he was more than halfway there already. Preston sat back, feeling the most at ease he had in months... and still oddly tense.

His fingers traced the old scar, an unconscious motion that came along with the memories. Getting questioned by law enforcement about Jagger and his family didn't always come with bruises or scars. Tonight hadn't, when FBI Agent Saunders had knocked on his hotel room door and respectfully implied that if Preston didn't turn on his best friend, there'd be hell to pay. He told Saunders that he'd been paying the devil for a long goddamned time and slammed the door in the guy's face...but not before noticing the world-weary look in the agent's eyes, like he'd seen too much.

Preston saw the same look in his own eyes every time he looked in the goddamned mirror, and he didn't want to have anything in common with Saunders. The agent was just another in a long line of people trying to fuck with Jagger through Preston. Supposedly, the King family was on FBI, DEA, and ATF watch-lists, and those were working to build a RICO case against them, which would include racketeering charges.

All Preston knew was that he'd never let himself be the reason his best friend got taken down.

"*One of these days, Preston? You're going to need a bargaining chip —and I'll be it.*"

"*I'm never going to need shit from you, Saunders.*" That's when he'd walked over toward the highway and called Jagger.

Jagger, who was at present pulling into a Wendy's drive-thru lane and ordering half the goddamned menu. "Your stomach was growling. Must've been all that thinking."

Preston didn't say anything until Jagger had pulled around to the window and collected their food. The rain was coming down hard again, so Jagger pulled into a spot in the back lot while they ate.

Finally, Preston crumpled the wrapper from his burger and said, "An FBI agent came to my hotel tonight."

Jagger's jaw tightened, but he refused to look at Preston. "That didn't take long. Sorry."

"I wasn't sleeping before that happened anyway." Preston tried to make light of it. But Jagger's family business always hung between them, an invisible barrier. A shield. Something Jagger needed to protect Preston from.

"Your could've used the time to catch up on all the correspondence you missed."

"I keep up just fine."

"Not with me."

"I read and listened to all your messages," Preston corrected, trying to ignore Jagger's accusing tone.

"You just didn't acknowledge or answer them."

Because I didn't know how to say what I needed. But instead of telling Jagger that, he shot back, "You said you weren't coming alone."

"You told me not to. I didn't answer. And I see you're still good at changing the subject."

"You're determined to start a fight. I figured I'd choose the topic."

When Jagger murmured, "Asshole," Preston finally felt like they were back on even ground.

"You need to know that, no matter what, I'll do time before I let him—or any of them—touch you or your family," Preston growled.

"I'd walk into the station and surrender myself before I let that happen. They've got nothing."

"I know it's all bullshit. I can deal with it."

"You shouldn't have to." Jagger's hand went to his shoulder. "Did he touch you?"

"No," Preston said quickly, swore his cheekbone throbbed.

As if reading his mind, Jagger ran a fingertip along the barely there —and forever reminder of their bond—scar. "That's the day I knew."

"Knew what?"

"That we were ride or die."

Preston wanted to ask so many questions. About the kiss. His confusion. How Jagger could be both angry with him and still love him...because in Preston's family, anger wasn't love. But his throat tightened and his ears rang, and somehow, he was here with Jagger and back on the battlefield at the same time.

It wasn't until they were almost back to Vintage Ridge that Preston could breathe normally again. That was when Jagger told him, "I've got to tell you something. I've been getting threats—that's nothing new, but they're specific to the club."

Protection was Preston's wheelhouse. He never backed down from danger. "What kind of threats?"

"What do you think, Pres? The usual—from the people who aren't happy about my father giving up his business. People who aren't happy I'm taking over and changing things. Same day, same shit."

"Why are you so damned casual about this?"

"Because I grew up knowing it would happen. So did you—you can't tell me you're surprised."

"Not really, no." Preston stared out at the dark, rainy stretch of road in front of them that would lead them to Rúnda. *Home.*

Jagger absently tapped the edge of his ring against the steering wheel, a longstanding habit he'd had from the time he'd first gotten the heavy metal with his family's crest on it at the age of sixteen. It had looked big back then, and so unfamiliar on Jagger's hand. Jagger had grown into it quickly, and now, his hand would've seemed empty without it.

"These are the first threats I've gotten since the club's opening last year."

"Is this you trying to talk me into working security for you?"

"Fuck you, Pres. It's me telling you about the threats so you can decide if you want to stay with me or not. It's not as safe as it once was."

"It was never safe." Preston hadn't given a shit about that, not when they were younger and definitely not now. "Stay with you? Or work for you?"

"Both. And it's working *with* me, not *for* me."

"Right." Preston wouldn't walk away from Jagger—not now, with the threats. But it would be tricky as fuck with the FBI wanting him to turn on Jagger. Preston had been hoping to keep some distance between them.

Should've thought about that before you grabbed Jagger and kissed him, you straight asshole.

"So, you'll consider it seriously? Working with me?" Jagger's voice interrupted his reverie.

"Are you going to listen to my security recommendations, and implement them, no matter what?"

"Of course."

"Like you listened to me about not coming alone tonight?"

"That's different."

"Different how? Because you listened but did exactly what you wanted to do anyway? You'll make it impossible for any security detail to help you. If you want to be a one-man show, go for it. If you really want help—"

"I want your help, Pres. I trust you."

Preston felt like he'd won a small victory from the stubborn man.

"I want to check out security at the club, and I'll have your back while I'm figuring things out."

"Were you thinking of doing something else?"

Preston shrugged. "I don't think they're going to let me out—not fully, anyway." He was too well trained, had cost the military far too much money to simply be allowed to walk away from his Green Beret days.

"So what—are you officially part of the National Guard?"

"Something like that. They call and I jump."

"With no notice." Jagger sounded resigned but not surprised.

"I'll make sure you're covered."

"That's not...dammit, Preston." Jagger hit the steering wheel with his palm. "It didn't have to be like this. It never had to be like this. You didn't have to run to enlist in the first place."

"I wasn't running, Jagger. I needed to fucking establish myself. Or I really would've been what my family called me."

"Jagger's whore?" he bit out. "You refused to let anyone pay your way. Don't they know that?"

"It didn't matter. They knew you'd offered to take care of me—you and your family. They didn't understand it then, and now—"

"This isn't the same."

"Feels like it can be."

"Dammit, you know what kind of security I need. And you're in the unique position of already being trusted to provide it."

Preston pressed the heels of his palms to his eyes. "I told you I'd consider it. That I'd help you in the meantime. Can that be enough for now? I'm working on two hours of sleep here."

"Yeah," Jagger said roughly. "It's always enough when you're here."

Jagger

Finally, Jagger pulled the Suburban into the alleyway behind the club, ignoring the fact that this was where all hell had broken loose between them a year ago, during Rúnda's opening week. The brick wall was where Preston had backed him up and kissed him. Kissed him like there was no going back, hands fisted in Jagger's hair to hold him in place, moaning into Jagger's mouth as their bodies did a slow, dirty grind.

He glanced over at Preston, who was also staring at the brick wall. Jagger forced himself to turn away and open the back door instead, and then Preston followed him inside and up the stairs to the apartment.

"Looks great up here. You've done a lot of work since last time."

"Not that much." He stared at Preston under the soft lights. "Need anything else? A drink?"

Preston shook his head. "I'm good—just tired."

"Come on, then, let's go to bed." Jagger began to strip as he headed toward the bedroom, the way he always did. There was no sense in acting differently. The more comfortable he acted, the more comfortable Preston would ultimately be. And Preston did follow him into the bedroom, dropped his bag, and stripped to his underwear before crawling under the sheets on the left side of the bed where he always slept.

At this point, Jagger only slept on the right side of the bed. "How's it feel to be somewhat of a free man?"

Preston stared at the ceiling and smiled. "Odd. Like I'm not attached to anything."

Jagger knew how Preston was feeling—untethered. Flying blind. Unmoored. The Army could still call on him, but it was no longer part of Preston's daily life beyond keeping himself in shape. Preston would've trained hard either way. "I've got you, kid."

"Fuck off with that kid shit—you're only a few months older." Preston turned onto his side, his back facing Jagger.

"But so much wiser." He slung an arm around Preston before half curling, protectively, around his friend. Because he knew Preston hated to ask, the same way he knew his friend's nightmares were nearly nonexistent when they slept this way. "You're home with me. Safe."

"Safe," Preston murmured, like the word was foreign to him.

CHAPTER THREE

Preston

WHENEVER PRESTON WAS WITH JAGGER, he went right back to being in high school again, pulled between two worlds. Preston's parents had ultimately—and unwittingly—contributed to his friendship with Jagger by putting him into a tough Boston public school after he'd purposely failed out of the fancy prep schools they'd continued to shove him in. It was supposed to shock him into understanding how good he'd had it, but it did the exact opposite. Because Jagger's father and brother and uncles became more of a family to him than his own had ever been.

Both their families had money, but the Kings' money was far more unacceptable than the VanValen's blue-blooded fortune. And when Preston's family issued him the ultimatum that, once he graduated high school, he needed to pick being disowned and losing his trust or Jagger? Preston had picked Jagger, and the Army, in that order.

Jagger offered Preston the world when he was disowned. Preston refused, knowing he'd needed to make his own way. He'd gone from Army grunt to Ranger to Green Beret...and now, he was back with Jagger, with law enforcement still harassing him and his parents sure to follow. And Jagger? Was still trying to take care of him.

He could still hear his mother calling him *Jagger's whore*. He shifted restlessly, hating that memory.

"You all right?" Jagger murmured.

"Sorry—yeah. Just trying to get comfortable. I didn't mean to wake you."

"I wasn't asleep," Jagger told him, his arm banding more tightly around Preston, which was confusing and still somehow necessary.

They'd started sleeping like this early on in his Army career. He'd come home on leave and found sleep an impossibility. The nightmares had gotten worse over the years, thanks to his childhood and the now-ten years of combat which included several near misses, a couple of direct hits, and a near capture.

The dreams were a motherfucker, woke him up yelling, looking for a weapon that Jagger thankfully wouldn't let him have when he was home. And then Jagger would guide him back to bed and stay with him for the rest of the night. That was what happened on his first and second leaves. By the third, Jagger was lying next to him in bed from the start, grounding him, and Preston's nightmares substantially improved.

After a long moment, he surprised Preston by asking, "Are you seeing anyone?"

"Fucked my way through all the women along the Eastern Seaboard," Preston said tiredly, finally safe in the dark. *And could only see your face.* "Nothing serious. You?"

"I still have a few regulars."

But Preston knew that was different than seeing someone. Jagger did scenes. Had regulars he saw weekly, but he didn't have a single, permanent sub. Still, he forced himself to ask, "Anyone serious?" just in case.

Jagger's weight pressed closer. "No."

He almost let *good* slide out of his mouth, but instead he brushed his cheek against the pillow. For now, Jagger's *no* was the only comfort he needed. "Thanks."

"For what?"

"Rescuing me."

Jagger snorted softly. "You're no damsel in distress."

"That's your job, I guess."

Jagger laughed and tightened his grip around Preston.

Less than twelve hours after sleeping next to Jagger in his bed, Preston sat next to him at Rúnda's bar watching him get half mauled by another guy.

Jagger was bi and a Dom, so it's not like he minded it, and hell, this was a BDSM club, where hookups were pretty much guaranteed. Men like the younger one pawing at Jagger were carefully accepted into the club on a trial basis as guests of members before being allowed to come in on their own. And Preston was straight, and none of this had ever been a problem for him before.

But it was most definitely bothering him now—the way it had bothered him last time he'd been here.

It wasn't just about this guy—it was everything. The memories of the kiss. This whole club. It was Jagger. And what the hell was he supposed to do with a sudden, inexplicable, undeniable sexual pull toward his best friend?

How about not kissing him and then running, for starters. Or trying to pretend that watching gay porn for the last year and jerking off to Jagger hadn't been happening?

He told himself to shut up.

This guy perving on Jagger didn't look like some kind of exclusive member. Preston was in charge of security, so it wouldn't be too extra if he ran a background check. Immediately. In fact, he was trying to figure out a way to quietly pocket the man's glass so he could run his prints, at the very least, when Jagger slid a shot in front of him.

"Have a drink, Pres." Jagger's voice sounded rough, and he winked before turning back to his conquest.

He knew what Preston was thinking—about the fingerprints, and, for all Preston knew, about everything. The air had changed between them, the current charged. But Jagger had left the ball solidly in Preston's court, never more so than with this last shot.

Jagger had always been kinky—Preston knew that. He'd watched Jagger pick up men in various clubs, and he'd listened through thin walls when Jagger had company. Harnesses, cuffs, dildos...those were always lying around Jagger's place, and Jagger was always encouraging him to find someone to try them out with.

"New horizons," Jagger had suggested.

Preston recalled shaking his head. "I don't need all this to get laid."

"Dude, you have no idea what you're missing."

And Preston hadn't...until he'd accidentally walked into a dungeon room exhibition, starring Jagger. In leather pants which left nothing to the imagination, tattoos on full display, and enough sexual prowess to make everyone observing want him.

It was one thing to hear Jagger talk about his sessions, see the sex toys in his bedroom, but it was quite another to witness the public goings-on in the private space. Thinking about what else happened when a man or woman was led from the floor into one of the dungeon rooms was what had gotten Preston into this trouble in the first place.

Because being around it had turned Preston on, something he hadn't wanted to admit. Turned him on to *Jagger*, for Christ's sake. If he'd found himself attracted to a random club guy, it probably wouldn't have bothered him so much.

But watching Jagger be attracted to a random club guy? Annoying as fuck. So Preston glared at the younger man who was practically sitting on Jagger's lap and watched his best friend smile affectionately.

"I don't really have limits," the guy was telling Jagger.

"Everyone has limits." Jagger ran a finger along the guy's throat. "I like finding—and exploiting them."

"Then you should take me to a room, tie me up, and leave me at your mercy."

Preston fought a growl, downed two shots, and motioned for a third. They might as well've been water for all the good they did him.

Jagger definitely noticed the tension, but he hadn't stopped the guy from half climbing into his lap, and so Preston was actually relieved when his phone rang.

Less so when he realized who was calling.

Without glancing back at Jagger, he left the bar area to take the call outside, not bothering with a hello when he picked up. "I told you I didn't want to hear from you."

His father countered with, "I told you that you didn't have a choice."

Preston learned a long time ago that actively fighting his family didn't work. Escaping to the military had given him momentary repose, but now that he was out, he was unsurprised that their threats had begun anew. "I already told Agent Saunders exactly what I was prepared to do."

"Which was absolutely nothing." His father sounded angry, which pleased Preston. Usually the man remained calm and cold as ice. "Where are you now?"

"I'm betting you already know the answer to that."

"You ran to him already." His father paused. "Your mother and I are prepared to cooperate with Agent Saunders. I know you think I don't have any leverage, but that's not true. I'll do anything in my power to get you away from that family. You know I always keep my word."

Preston hung up the phone, knowing his father had already cut the call off. His family was always attempting to follow through on their promise to ruin Jagger's family, something they'd done steadily since that first day when Jagger had walked him home. Preston would've pointed out that his parents were the ones who'd sent him to that public school, but honestly, that had been his doing. He'd purposely failed out of every prep school they'd put him in, until they'd stuck him in a tough southie school to purposely teach him a lesson.

And Preston had, just not the lesson his father had hoped.

"You've humiliated this family over and over again, Preston. You'll learn too late where you belong."

Preston knew exactly where he belonged, had felt it the first time he'd climbed into Jagger's car, the first time he'd been welcomed into the King family home. He'd always assumed his father's hatred of them was because they weren't blue-bloods, weren't elite. It seemed irrational, but so did everything his father did when it came to him.

The only thing for Preston to do now was make sure that the club —and Jagger—were as safe as possible. Sticking around for longer than a visit here or there could bring big trouble for Jagger.

Preston's family had a long reach, political connections, and even though Sean King was never afraid of them, Preston needed to find a permanent solution to stop his parents from interfering. He also had to help Jagger deal with the threats, which was a hard thing to do when he wasn't allowed to listen to them. Jagger had insisted he just know that it was a threat to Jagger and the club, but anything more could leave Preston open to having to lie to law enforcement.

He couldn't work on wiring the club while it was open, in case he set an alarm off. He thought about going back into the bar area but quickly rejected that idea. And since he knew Jagger would be busy tonight, and the thought of sleeping alone wasn't appealing either. The fucked-up thing was, if Preston just said the word, Jagger would drop the guy he was flirting with and he'd stay with Preston.

Screw it. He'd catch a couple of movies and crash on the couch until Jagger came back. He threaded through the back hallways, which, like the rest of the club, had a dark, sleek, modern vibe. Dangerous-looking, much like Jagger himself. Even for Preston, it gave him a little thrill walking through the door. The exclusivity of it. The forbidden nature of the private, exclusive membership. The knowledge of what went on here, especially in the dungeon rooms.

This was a different level of protection added for the kink community that could possibly impact their business dealings. Preston knew politicians and judges had memberships here, and that Jagger didn't ask special favors—the only protection afforded any of the members was the insulation of their private life.

The dungeon provided even more protection. He automatically glanced at the blue room as he walked by. It was one of two private rooms on this floor, with the other three being on basement level. The blue room was the least intimidating, the one for the newer inductees into the kink scene.

The one he'd watched Jagger perform in.

"Pres! I heard you were back." Shara, one of the Doms who worked here was calling. She was tall and lithe and gorgeous, and had men and women following her around the club anytime Preston had seen her. They'd shared a flirtation when he was in town, but since he hadn't been into the scene and wasn't looking for any kind of commitment, he wanted to keep things friendly.

"Got in late last night," he told her as she leaned in and planted a kiss on his cheek without trying to embrace him. Preston didn't know if Jagger gave instructions that Preston hated to be touched post-combat or if they were all just sensitive to personal space because of the nature of their jobs, but he appreciated it all the same.

The intercom outside the green room flicked on for several seconds, and Preston was immediately surrounded by the long, loud groan of a man who sounded like he was being tortured and yet somehow enjoying it.

Each room was soundproofed, but there were intercoms for anyone who wanted to listen—if that's what the sub decided on ahead of time. Obviously, this sub had.

Now, Preston fought the shudder than ran through him and found Shara watching him intently.

"Still curious?" she asked, piggybacking on a conversation they'd had the last time he'd been on leave. He'd been drinking. Asking her questions about the dungeon, after seeing Jagger's performance. All of that happened before he'd kissed Jagger.

If Shara knew anything about that last part, she didn't let on. And lying to himself wasn't getting him goddamned anywhere. "Sometimes, yeah," he admitted finally. "Sometimes I wonder why I'm holding out."

Shara stared at him like she knew exactly what his problem was. Or maybe that's just what he wanted to believe.

"I watched you watching Jagger with that guy last time you were here," she told him, and he did not want to think about that at all—and yet, his brain had it on a continuous loop. "This stuff can bring up some pretty intense feelings."

"I'm not—it's not..."

"Preston, it's okay. Last time we talked you told me you'd never tried any of this." She motioned toward the dungeon rooms. "Did that change? Have you tried anything BDSM related at all?"

"Not really. Nothing like what happens here."

"Do you want to try it?"

"With Jagger?" he asked, before he could help himself.

Shara gave him a soft, knowing smile. "With me. You can pretend I'm anyone. Just between us, okay?"

Fuck, it'd been so long since he'd allowed himself any kind of sexual release that he found himself following her. Watching Jagger made him feel heavy. Drugged. And more turned-on than he could remember. He kept flashing back to their kiss, their make-out, their slow, dirty grind against each other in the rain...

Shara's voice broke into his reverie. "I'm free tonight—my session canceled. So I've got this big empty room and plenty of time and patience."

Which was how Preston ended up strapped, facedown, to a leather bench, wearing pink leather, fur-lined cuffs.

"This isn't going to work," Preston said, his throat dry as he glanced up at his bound wrists.

"Sugar, it's going to work out just fine. Please—relax and just promise me you'll give it a try."

The most ironic part of all of this was that Preston was thinking about doing exactly what Jagger had wanted him to do last time he'd been on leave. The conversation was etched finely into his memory.

"I think you should see Shara."

"Like take her on a date?"

"Like let her take you into the dungeon and whip the tension out of you."

"That's not my thing."

"Maybe it should be. Christ, you're spinning. Tense. When's the last time you got laid?"

"We all know the last time you did," Preston shot back, not sure what that had to do with anything. But it did—it had to do with everything. "This isn't my scene."

"You seem interested."

"Yeah, when it's happening to someone else."

"I've booked you a session with Shara. If nothing else, you can get your rocks off with her. It's a safe environment."

"You hired someone to have sex with me?"

"She offered—she thinks you're hot."

Obviously Shara had been watching Preston more closely than he'd thought.

Now, he felt her hands on him, had heard her mention "green, red, and yellow," and he knew that he could get out of these restraints if he really tried. He knew she was going light on him, as she'd called it.

Her strong hand palmed his bare ass and squeezed it, like she wanted his full attention, and hell, she had it now. "Like I mentioned earlier, sometimes, the men—or women—I'm with pretend I'm someone else. Someone they wish they could be with. I'm betting you've got someone in mind. All you need to do is relax. Enjoy. Pretend I'm the person you've been wanting. Call out their name if you want to, okay? This is a safe space. It's just us. I promise."

He felt himself nod, and when the pleasure started in earnest, the only name on his lips was Jagger's.

CHAPTER FOUR

Jagger

JAGGER HADN'T AGREED to a session with the guy Preston had been shooting looks at down by the bar. Instead, he'd begged off the man's company when Preston walked away, because it wasn't fun without Preston there to sulk.

When Stuart found him in the office, going over the numbers, he'd walked over to him and put a palm on Jagger's forehead.

Jagger lifted his head and glared. "The fuck, Stu?"

"Catching up on business on a Saturday night? You must be sick."

Jagger frowned and Stuart withdrew his hand and settled into the chair on the other side of the old desk. It'd been his father's, and Jagger wanted it here, even though it was completely out of place with the rest of the modern decor.

It was tradition. Good luck. The safety of childhood, watching his father sitting here, night after night.

"So...you and Preston seem...odd," Stuart offered.

Jagger flicked his gaze up. "Do you have a problem with him being here?" Preston and Stuart had never gotten on all that well. There'd never been any all-out brawl, although they'd gotten close more than a time or two. They represented two different factions of Jagger's life, and Stuart had always been wary of outsiders. Jagger had punched him the first and last time Stuart had called Preston that in front of Jagger, but it didn't change how Stuart felt.

"Not at all. I just figured things might improve with some breathing room." His unspoken "but they haven't" hung between them. "But now...I'm just surprised at his sudden interest in the club facilities is all."

"He's interested for security reasons."

"Oh."

"What are you trying to tell me?" Jagger demanded at Stuart's most unconvincing performance.

"Nothing. Nothing," Stuart repeated insistently, then paused. "It's just..."

"Stu, come on. Talk to me. You've got something to say about Preston, just say it."

"I do, but it's not what you're thinking. Just go look in on the blue room, okay? And you didn't hear it from me. I got rid of security already."

Jagger frowned. Was Preston in the blue room? A dungeon room?

Within seconds, he was letting himself into the secret space designed to oversee the dungeon rooms, for both safety and voyeur purposes. Normally, there would be someone stationed in here all night during business hours, but this room was empty, as Stuart had promised.

Preston was on the other side of the thick, one-way glass. He was buckled in, facedown, to a leather bench with Shara's pink, fur-lined leather cuffs around his wrists and ankles. She'd spanked him—his ass was red with her handprints, and he was alternately shuddering and obviously, even without the benefit of sound on, asking for more.

And Jagger wanted to break in there and give it to him.

Instead, he flipped the switch so he could hear, and Preston's strong moans immediately filled the room. Jagger swore he could smell his friend, wanted to walk in there and lick up the come he knew was already dripping from Preston's cock.

It was wrong of him to watch, to invade Preston's privacy, but fuck it all, there was no way Jagger could tear himself away. He was frozen to the spot, watching Shara do to Preston what he'd been dreaming about doing to him for years. Watched Shara slick her gloved finger with lube and slide it inside of Preston as he begged for it not to stop… looking so goddamned perfect all stretched out, skin slick with sweat, muscles standing out in stark definition.

It's not sex—it's just a grounding, Jagger repeated to himself.

There was nothing wrong with what Preston was doing…except for his choice of partner. In Jagger's opinion, his best friend's reactions told the entire truth—that Preston wanted—needed—more.

A strong need to possess Preston for himself surged through him, and Jagger was surprised he'd been able to stop himself from breaking the door down and taking Preston himself. Finishing him off with those goddamned, deceptively strong, pink fur cuffs holding him in place.

Instead, Jagger freed his own cock and stroked it until he came… which happened the second Preston called out, "Jagger!"

"Christ," he muttered, his body heavy and unsteady. He managed to switch off the intercom, because he didn't want to watch Shara perform aftercare. It was necessary, but Jagger's jealousy wouldn't allow it. Barely allowed him to sit here, cock out, waiting for the room to clear. Only when he was sure Preston was back upstairs did he walk out of the room.

Of course, Shara was waiting for him.

"Preston's bi," she informed him as she breezed past. "That was the hottest scene I've done in a long time. Think he'll come back?"

Not for you. "Maybe," he managed to grunt out. Barely.

Shara winked. "I saved a lot of firsts for you. If you finally decide to do something about it."

"Do you remember who you work for?"

"Do you know who owns your heart?" she shot back.

When he didn't answer, she simply laughed and walked away.

Preston

After leaving Shara, Preston limped upstairs to Jagger's loft and into the bathroom, where he spent ten spaced-out minutes staring at his reddened ass in the mirror before actually getting into the shower. Finally, he crawled into Jagger's bed. A glance at his phone told him that it was just after two in the morning.

A couple of hours of sleep and he'd normally be good as new... except that sleep wasn't happening. Instead, his ass throbbed, reminding him of what he'd done, and so he just tossed and turned without the benefit of having Jagger there. Knowing where Jagger was —and what he was doing—didn't help matters.

Then again, having Jagger close to him right now would probably be a huge mistake.

He'd ignored his ringing phone earlier, and now, when he checked his messages, he listened to his mother ranting about Jagger. Nothing had changed. The fact that Jagger was bisexual only added to her fury. She acted as if being around him could turn Preston, and the timing of her call wasn't lost on him. She was wrong about the turning part...but still, Preston couldn't deny that somewhere along the way he'd started wanting to fuck his best friend.

The love? Well, that'd been there from the start, albeit in a much different form than what he was feeling now. He might not know what to do with these new, burgeoning feelings, but what he did know was that Jagger was *his*. That possessive fierceness grew every time he was in Jagger's presence, and it threatened to become so big and over-whelming that soon there'd be no hiding it.

His earlier orgasms hadn't satiated him—instead, the whole scene left him feeling overwhelmed and confused. So he gave up on sleeping completely and prepared to content himself with Netflix, until Jagger rolled in a few minutes later, going straight for the shower.

The jealousy hit Preston as sharply as a knife to the gut, and he shut the TV off and curled up around himself.

That only served to make Jagger tighten his body around Preston's when he finally did crawl into bed, smelling like body wash and sham-poo. "Are you in pain, Pres?"

More than you know. "I don't think I can work for you."

"You're working with me, not for me," Jagger said tiredly.

"It's not going to work."

Maybe Jagger heard something in his voice because his friend's next words were tense, full of unresolved anger. "Is this because I wasn't here to be your blankie?"

"Fuck you." Preston rolled away and started to get up, but Jagger had him by the throat, which was a risky-as-fuck move. Preston had never reacted well to being touched like that, and in a swift, sudden motion, he ended up on top of Jagger, staring down into his friend's dark eyes.

He'd never hurt Jagger. Never. But something in Preston's eyes must've worried Jagger enough to have him putting his hands up in surrender. And then the realization of how damned close they were, how easy it would be to lean in and kiss Jagger again had Preston simply staring...with Jagger staring back up at him.

Finally, Preston eased off him with a clipped "Sorry" before he moved to sit on the edge of the bed, unable to close his eyes against an onslaught of memories. Unwilling to keep them open either—reality was too damned much.

"What the fuck happened tonight?" Jagger tried again.

"Doesn't matter. Decision's made." And it had never been a sure thing—Jagger had to know that. But between Preston's parents and Preston's feelings for Jagger, this was a land mine best left untouched.

"It matters to me." Jagger's voice rambled down his spine, a bourbon-drinking, hard-living voice that tugged at Preston.

"Why?"

"Don't make your decision based on—"

"My feelings?" Preston bit out. *You're still his whore.*

"You're still raw, Pres. You've been here just twenty-four hours. Please, give it at least another couple of weeks, at least."

Jagger was probably right.

But this time, Jagger being right might not help at all.

CHAPTER FIVE

Jagger

THE ONLY SAVING grace to Preston's silence was that tonight was poker night.

Jagger had been playing poker for as long as he could remember. His obsession with numbers, combined with his quick memory and attention to detail, made the game one of his favorites. He'd learned to play in his father's lap, and as a young teen, he'd been included in the adult games. Later in high school, he'd had his own game going on, with some friends and associates closer to his age.

It'd been a learning experience. He'd lost big and won big. But poker for him was a social sport, and Jagger had always been one to study people. It was what made him a good Dom, a good lover, and good at whatever jobs Sean King put him to.

Some had skated just this side of legal. Some he hadn't bothered to do more than deliver the message he'd been asked to and walk away. Along the way, his family became known for their ability to fix most things in their community. They had the gift of being able to soothe both sides, stop violence before it began—and start it when necessary.

But poker cut through all of that—it was a time and a place where he sat with colleagues and honed his skills and socialized. It had taken a bit of finagling to find the right balance for a monthly game, but they'd settled into a routine of six men, with two alternates. All of them were members of the club, which made sense.

Tonight, all the regulars—Trick, Diego, Doctor, Arthur, Skully—including him, would be here. They ranged from an MC Enforcer to a finance guy to the owner of an MMA training gym. They had a lawyer too...and Jagger himself, and they were all kinky fuckers. The only other people allowed were two bartender/waiters who were also regular staff members, to make sure everyone had drinks and food. The game tended to go until daybreak.

Which means Preston will sleep alone. Or not at all.

Preston, who'd been avoiding him all day by ripping out the old security system while simultaneously installing the new one.

It wasn't easy work, but Preston was obviously enjoying it. He didn't complain, or ask for help, and so Jagger left him alone for the majority of the day. Maybe Preston would clear his goddamned head enough to talk to Jagger about how he was feeling.

Jagger was the most sex- and kink-positive person he knew, so why wouldn't Preston talk to his about his choice of kink?

But you should be Preston's choice, the devil sitting on his shoulder murmured.

Dammit. He needed to get his mind clear or he was going to get crushed tonight. And seeing Preston half-naked in the room with the poker table did nothing to quell his fears. Or his cock.

He stood silently in the doorway, staring at his old friend's bare back and the way his ass looked in an old, worn pair of jeans. His hair was tied back and hidden under a bandanna, the way he'd often worn it in the military as per the pictures he'd send Jagger from time to time.

It was a good look on him, and Jagger admired the view for as long as he thought could get away with it.

Finally, Preston asked, "Did you need something?"

There were so many ways to go with that question, but Jagger took pity on him, especially when he noticed how tight Preston's shoulders were. "I was just coming down to set up for poker night. I didn't know you were still working—you've been at this for over twelve hours."

"You know I like keep busy. Plus, you need this done and soon," Preston told him, and yes, Jagger had heard Preston muttering all day about "this piece-of-shit old system." But he was more worried that Preston was hurrying this job along so he could make a run for it—again. "Wait—what poker night? I thought the club was closed on Mondays."

"It is. But the poker game's a monthly thing, and it's tonight."

Preston frowned. "I didn't know that was still a thing."

Because you haven't been here. Jagger had started it up almost as soon as he'd moved here so he could force himself to interact with some of the area's most prominent members. It was important for club business. It also helped him keep his ear to the ground, since North Carolina was brand-new territory for him. "Well, now you do."

Preston ground his teeth together. "You want me in charge of security, you need to tell me shit."

"I asked Stuart to give you an itinerary."

"You asked Stuart?" Preston walked toward him, stopping inches away. "You asked *Stuart* to give *me* an itinerary. That dumb fucker wouldn't piss on me if I was on fire, and you trust him to help me?"

Yeah, this was the old Preston. The one who took no shit and no prisoners. The one with the fire in his eyes. Jagger wanted to keep it there. "Do you want to repeat it one more time, or are you having trouble grasping the general concept of what I said?"

"Do you want me to shut down your little poker game over possible security breaches? Because that's about to happen."

Jagger narrowed his eyes. "You wouldn't do that."

"Do you really think I wouldn't do that?"

"I don't know, Preston. I'm sure there are things you do that would surprise me, even after all these years."

Preston seemed to move in a little closer, murmured, "Yeah, I'm sure there are things I do that would surprise even you."

Were they still even talking about poker? Did it matter? Because Jagger was ready to push Preston down and fuck him right here…

"Is there a problem?" Stuart asked from the doorway.

Preston swung his body away from Jagger. "You're the problem, Stuart. Always have been."

"The feeling's always been mutual, Preston." Stuart smiled and held up a paper. "I have tonight's itinerary for you right here. I didn't see you around earlier."

"How about I fix it so your eyes are too swollen to see anything for a couple of days?" Preston sneered, and Jagger thought about moving in between them.

"How about you try?" Stuart walked farther into the room and advanced on Preston, which was a definite mistake. Before Jagger could step in, the men were full out brawling, like they'd both suddenly realized that all the years of pent-up circling and small skirmishes had done shit…and in full view of Doctor and Trick, who stood there, obviously amused.

"I didn't know you'd be having entertainment," Doctor said with a smile, even as Trick's eyes roamed Preston's body, making Jagger want to rip the eyeballs from his sockets. The violence he felt must've been palpable, because Trick walked a wide circle around him to stand on the other side of the poker table as Preston and Stuart continued to roll around. Preston obviously had the upper hand, and Jagger knew there was no way he'd go much farther. He couldn't, had taken an oath not to fight civilians, because with his training, things could get ugly fast. Stuart was tough, but he wouldn't be any match for the kind of skills Preston had learned in the last ten years.

"Enough," Jagger growled, his voice low. He heard Preston curse, watched him push away from Stuart like he'd been burned. Like he was pissed he'd lost control that easily. Stuart, on the other hand, seemed happy enough to have caused the trouble, despite the blood dripping from his nose.

Preston's face appeared to have come through mainly unscathed. "Go shove the itinerary up your nose to stop the bleeding, Stuart," he suggested.

Stuart shot him the finger, spit blood onto the paper before crumpling it up and disappeared with it. Preston grabbed his T-shirt and pulled it on.

"Are we going to have a problem?" Jagger asked, his voice low.

"I'll let you know," Preston promised before following Stuart out of the room...and walking past a very interested Diego, Arthur, and Skully.

"Who is he?" Doctor finally asked. Doctor really was a doctor, but he wasn't a "Doc" type. No, he was three-piece suits, always put together, operating on the wealthy, and refusing to take insurance kind of doctor. But despite his various pretensions, he'd been a good friend to Jagger and the others over the years. He liked his kink and his poker, and he paid his debts. He also refused to talk to the police about Jagger or any of the men he sat with, month after month. As far as Jagger knew, he wasn't into anything illegal, but he didn't doubt that Doctor had his hand in something. Rumors surrounding him were anything from money laundering to illegal organ transplants.

Honest, innocent men rarely came here...except for Preston. But he was an entirely different story, which was why a sense of unease settled over Jagger at Doctor's seemingly innocent question.

Trick glanced over before Jagger did. Trick was a biker with the Hangmen MC—the club's Enforcer—and a longtime acquaintance. He'd been especially helpful when Jagger was scouting locations. "That's Preston—he's with Jagger."

Jagger didn't bother to correct that, simply added, "He's upgrading the security system."

"Anything we should worry about?" Doctor asked.

"He just says the old system's shit," Jagger told him. "He's a perfectionist. And I trust him implicitly."

Doctor raised his brows but simply nodded at Jagger's assertion. "This is a very promising start." Doctor sat back and crossed a leg at the angle. "Calls for cigars, at the very least. So, let's get to it."

CHAPTER SIX

Preston

PRESTON RIPPED the itinerary out of Stuart's hand and didn't feel a damned bit guilty about the man's impending black eye. "Go put some ice on that or you won't be able to see in the morning," he instructed instead, planting himself behind Jagger's desk.

He glanced at the paperwork, which laid out three months' worth of plans for the club, including special parties, membership recruitments, and yes, the monthly poker games.

Christ. He scanned the list of names, not recognizing any of them except Trick's. He'd met the Hangmen MC member when the club first opened. Having a high-ranking member of a notorious, one-percenter motorcycle club hanging around was a definite risk for Trick and Jagger alike, since the various alphabet agencies had their eyes on both men. Still, there were far worse security risks for Jagger to have in and around the club, and Trick was probably a good man to have his back. Or Jagger's back.

He'd been waiting for Jagger to tell him to fuck off, but to his credit, Jagger had been his usual mouthy self without trying to take away any of the authority he'd given Preston.

Preston ran the names through a database that wouldn't dig too deeply and throw out any red flags, and he learned enough about each of the men to satisfy himself that none of them would kill Jagger tonight, at least. He had no doubt that all the men were carrying weapons though, and that was something he'd need to change for the next poker game.

If you're still here.

But while he was here, he needed to get back into the room where the men with weapons were. He walked in, without knocking, ignoring the slight pause of the game. He'd finish wiring the room while they played, effectively killing two birds with one stone.

He stood by the opened electrical panel, his back to the table, and worked as he listened. They'd probably already asked Jagger about him, but Preston didn't doubt they'd have more to say now that he was present.

He wasn't disappointed.

The men were all raising one another with money that made Preston's brows rise, which wasn't unusual for Jagger's poker games. Preston was a frequent visitor slash witness to his games, mainly to admit Jagger's skill with numbers. Tonight was no exception, with Jagger winning several hands in a row.

That was when the man called Doctor said, "Let's up the ante."

"What do you have in mind?" Trick asked. "Table stakes?"

"We're not playing pro—it's just a friendly game," Doctor pointed out, his tone anything but friendly. "Let's sweeten the pot...with Preston."

Preston continued wiring, his fingers instinctively knowing what to do while his mind froze and he pretended he didn't hear a goddamn word. As the seconds of silence ticked by, he waited for Jagger to tell Doctor to fuck off.

Until it became apparent he'd be waiting forever.

"Preston's the pot?" the lawyer named Arthur asked, sounding far too intrigued for Preston's taste. "Maybe someone should clear it with him, then?"

"I thought I'd clear it with Jagger," Doctor said.

Preston forced himself to pull wires calmly, like the outcome of the conversation didn't matter to him at all. It was in Jagger's hands now, and Preston respected that while knowing there was no graceful way for Jagger to decline the doctor's suggestion without looking unsure of his abilities...in all areas. That fucking prick Doctor knew it too.

Just because Jagger had asserted that Preston was his didn't mean he couldn't share. That happened between Doms and their subs often enough, Preston knew.

But Jagger wasn't his Dom.

"I think you should ask Preston—his scene, his rules. I don't run him," Jagger said calmly, echoing Preston's thoughts.

Preston realized that he wanted Jagger to lay claim to him, which was ridiculous.

"Is he straight?" Diego, the MMA gym owner Dom, asked now.

"They all claim to be until they get into a dungeon room with one of us," Trick pointed out, and everyone laughed. Except Preston, who wavered between kicking everyone at the table's ass...or just Jagger's, for putting him in this position.

"One shirtless fight and this happens? Christ, you guys are easy. Or hard up," Preston said, his attention still on the wires. He heard most of the men laugh, but Jagger didn't.

When Preston finally turned around, he couldn't place the look in Jagger's eyes, but he could feel the tension strung between them as if electrically charged. Did the other men notice it as well?

"Come on, Preston—make it fun," Trick begged. "I'm dying of boredom over here, and not just because I'm losing."

Jagger shook his head at Preston, an almost imperceptible *no*. A warning. A *don't do it or else*. A flush of anger heated him, and the words came out of his mouth before he could stop them. "I'm in. But whoever wins better make it good."

"I will, Preston," Doctor promised.

"I wouldn't get your hopes up." Jagger's voice was couched in an easy cadence.

"Something will definitely be up when I'm done with him," Doctor added. Preston didn't doubt that some of these men were straight, but based on the background search, most of them were either Doms or tops who would take on members of their own sex for a session...but not necessarily involve sex in the mix. He'd seen it happen time and time again, both in this club and in the others he'd gone to with Jagger.

Thankfully, one of the waiters walked in just then, bearing more drinks and food.

"Perfect timing. Let's take a break before we resume play." Jagger got up from the table. "Preston, with me."

Preston followed him, aware that all the men were watching. "Why would you—"

"Why would I?" Jagger's voice was low and dangerous. "The pot never stays in the room when we're playing. Got it?"

He swallowed, hard. "Fine."

"What the fuck, Pres? You had an out. You just say 'no' or 'I'm not interested,' or 'I'm not into the scene...' because you're not, *right?*"

Something in Jagger's piercing gaze made Preston want to confess everything right there...but everything in Jagger's tone made Preston also want to tell him to fuck off. "You don't run me, remember? And pain's just weakness leaving the body and all that shit, *right?*"

Jagger's dark look made him take a step back, and he ended up hitting the wall. "You really need to be taken in hand."

"Then you'll have to win," Preston shot back. He'd meant it to come out as a joke, but it sounded nothing of the sort.

It wasn't smart to taunt Jagger, but Preston was too angry still to care. His ass still ached, and he was still twitchy from last night and his reaction to what Shara did to him.

For him.

"I always win, Preston. I thought you knew that about me by now." There was something about the look in his best friend's eye that made Preston feel more like prey than Doctor had...because Jagger wore that same expression Preston had seen countless times, although it had never, ever been directed at him.

Or had it been?

He shifted subtly, but Jagger's gaze locked on his before he smiled, and not that warm, affectionate smile.

Preston could hear Jagger's order as clearly as if he'd spoken out loud—one he often gave to the men who subbed for him in the club.

You're in trouble, boy.

Preston wasn't sure he was going to like the lesson he was about to be taught at all.

Jagger

Jagger had never expected Doctor to involve Preston...at least not this soon out of the gate. But Preston was now a part of this world, and so Doctor saw him as fair game.

Because you didn't clarify who—what—Preston was to you.

Instead of feeling guilty, Jagger focused on remaining calm, because resistance and anger would just cloud his judgment. He had a poker hand to win.

Preston was dangerous in his own right, but in Jagger's world, there were rules. Preston needed to get his sea legs and learn his place.

Show no weakness, Jagger.

As the hours wore on, Jagger remained focused, until finally, he won the final hand and the entire round. His hand was one of the best he'd had in a long goddamned time, and it was far more satisfying than it should've been. He put his cards down, Doctor *tsked*, Trick cursed, and Jagger told them, "You're all assholes."

"Let's not pretend you haven't wanted this for years," Doctor said easily.

Jagger made a mental note to strangle Stuart in his sleep. Not like this."

"Too bad, you won, fair and square. I didn't lower my game because I definitely wanted his ass," Trick told him. "Now go get your boy."

"He's not—"

"Your boy," Doctor finished for him, reiterating Trick's point.

It took another hour or so before Jagger was locking up for the night, rearming the system that Preston somehow had working, despite the spiderweb of loose wires everywhere.

He found Preston waiting in his apartment, on the couch, watching TV. He was pretending to be calm, but Jagger could practically hear his heart beating. "Aren't you going to ask who won?"

Preston shrugged. "I'm waiting with bated breath for you to share."

Until that very moment, that very goddamned second, Jagger was planning on letting Preston completely off the hook. But with Preston pretending not to care, or worse, thinking that Jagger couldn't win? No.

He'd never planned on going through with it, not until Preston acted like it wasn't even a possibility, like they were still going to ignore that heart-stopping, near-friendship-ending kiss in the rain.

The one Preston had completely initiated, after a night out at Evoque, where they'd spent a night drinking and dancing, with everyone thinking they were together. Jagger preferred it that way, because then they were left alone. Together. And while he'd never expected Preston to shove him against the wall outside Rúnda and kiss him senseless, hands feathered in Jagger's hair, bodies grinding together, he certainly hadn't minded it. The rain had soaked them both, but the world around them stopped. For Jagger, the sky had split wide open and given him a goddamned gift.

He'd never expected it to split their friendship apart. And he'd be damned if he'd continue to let it do so.

"I won the pot," he told Preston now.

Preston rolled his eyes and scoffed. "Great. So I'm off the hook."

Many of the Doms Jagger knew didn't put sex on the table at all—for them, there was a pure line between what they did and who they slept with. It worked for them. It never really had for Jagger.

And he knew why.

"Why" was still staring at him with a deliberately blank expression.

Jagger was about to change that. "No, Pres—you're definitely not off the hook. We've got a date in the dungeon, tomorrow night at nine."

CHAPTER SEVEN

Preston

PRESTON STOOD as if Jagger's voice had the power to control him. "I'm not a sub." But his protest sounded hollow, even to his own ears.

"You don't have to be a sub in order to submit for a night. I figured you knew that already."

Preston didn't know anything anymore. "Let's slow down. Start over. I get you were trying to save me tonight."

"And I did. Save you, that is," Jagger said. Preston waited for him to add *again*, but he didn't and instead smiled, a dangerous smile. "It's going to happen, Pres. Let's not pretend a paddle and a finger don't turn you on. You looked pretty comfortable all tied up with a red ass and taking a finger to your hole."

Preston backed up as if Jagger's words had an actual bite to them. "What are you talking about?"

"I watched. I saw you, tied up. Moaning. Loving it." Jagger continued moving forward toward him predatorily, and Preston kept moving backward until he hit the wall. "I've also been watching you stare me down in the club every time someone else approaches me. Sometimes you get affectionate. Handsy. Or completely, outwardly jealous. Last year. Last night too."

Preston swallowed and tried to tell him that wasn't true, but he couldn't. Jagger had obviously been studying him, but all Preston could focus on was what Jagger had seen last night.

Jagger had watched Shara spread his ass cheeks and circle his hole with a lubed finger before pressing it inside, calling it his "tight pussy," and rubbing his dick like a clit.

"Want me to suck your tits while I fuck your sweet pussy with my fingers?" she'd asked, and when all he could do was moan, she'd done exactly that with strong strokes on his cock and he'd come, seeing stars.

Mainly, because he was pretending it was Jagger's hand. Jagger's voice. And how fucked-up was that?

"You're wrong," Preston managed, but his voice sounded thin and unsure.

"You don't want me, but you don't want anyone else to have me—is that it?"

"What? No."

"You don't sound too sure of yourself."

"You're too close."

"Tomorrow night, I'm going to be even closer." Jagger put a finger under his chin and forced Preston to meet his eyes.

"You've done this before? Played poker for a chance to fuck someone?"

"No one mentioned fucking specifically." Jagger kept his tone even. "And yes."

"Were they willing?"

"Were you?"

For you, he wanted to say. Instead, he played deliberately dumb. "I wanted to make you look good tonight."

Jagger smiled, like he knew why Preston ignored the question about being willing for Shara. "You trusted me. And I won. In the end, that's all that matters. Tomorrow, stop by Ace's Wild—it's a sex shop You need to buy a pair of pink fur-lined cuffs. And an anal hook."

"What the fuck?" Preston searched Jagger's face, waiting for the break in his expression, the joke that had to be lurking under all of this.

But Jagger was completely serious. "The blue room—tomorrow at 9:00 p.m., with your supplies."

The blue room at nine...the exact time and place Shara had booked for him.

Jagger confirmed his thoughts. "It worked out perfectly that Shara set that time aside for you."

"You're keeping track of my sex life?"

"*That's* your sex life?"

"Fuck. You." Preston shook his head. "What're you trying to do?"

"You said it yourself—you owe me. I decided to start listening to you."

"You're twisting my words."

Jagger tried to look innocent and completely failed. "My interpretation."

"You're a dick." Jagger just shrugged. "Fuck, it's me, Jag. *Me.* Your best friend."

"I know exactly who you are. That's not the problem."

A big game of chicken, and Jagger seemed unconcerned that Preston's dick was the prize. Preston stared at Jagger's bottomless dark eyes, wanting to see the same expression of affection he always had and not finding it.

Had Preston fucked this up completely? Was there no going back?

Why not go forward? But his throat tightened up too much to speak.

Finally, Jagger said, "Come to bed soon. You'll need a good night's sleep. For tonight, it's business as usual." With those words, Jagger strode off into the bedroom, and Preston stood gawking after him, wondering how anything in civilian life could've surprised him so much more than anything the battlefield had ever thrown at him.

Jagger heard you call out his name while you begged for more.

He blinked as flashes of Jagger bringing him to his first bar, first gay club, first fetish club flew through his mind, like someone was flipping pictures of his past too quickly. And none of it seemed weird because he was with Jagger, and he was cool with whatever made Jagger happy.

They were often mistaken for lovers at the club.

Jagger had been the one to drive him to the recruiter's office. And Jagger had dropped him off for basic training, had been waiting to pick him up for his first leave. And his next one. And the one after that...

They were connected.

To Preston? Jagger was simply his home.

And now, Jagger was threatening to take him apart, piece by piece, and Preston wasn't sure anyone would be able to put him back together after that. Nothing had been the same after Preston had kissed him. But all the milestones of his life up until this point had been filled with Jagger-sized markers.

This would prove to be no exception.

After a restless-as-fuck night's sleep with visions of Jagger tying him down and waking up with a vicious hard-on, Preston knew he'd have to get his visit to the sex shop over with if he was going to get anything else done that day. He was up long before Jagger, went for a long-assed run. Showered. Avoided Jagger and Stuart, who were holed up in Jagger's office by that point. Grabbed breakfast at the diner around the corner and finally, gave himself a pep talk on the way to Ace's Wild.

The shop was housed inside a brick building with white accents around the front window. The sign had handcuffs strategically placed to hang between the *s* and the *w*, and Preston's face flushed at the reminder of what he was going in there to buy. He parked in the back lot and entered through the low-visibility side entrance option, which he appreciated. It wasn't like he knew a lot of people in Vintage Ridge or he was particularly embarrassed by this, but he felt like he wore a neon sign that said, "I'm about to get fucked and spanked by my best friend."

It would've been better if Jagger had done so immediately following the poker game, but no, his friend knew how to drag out the sexual torture.

Preston wanted to get in and out of the sex shop fast, but hell, it wasn't like he knew his way around this place. He did know—immediately—that there was a lot of shit here that made his balls retract back inside his body and his dick flag. He could take pain, would never have made it as far as he had in his military career if he couldn't play hurt, but it didn't seem all that appealing to him during sex.

He walked around another corner and came upon a ripped black man with impressive dreads. He wore a Grateful Dead tie-dye shirt, was holding a giant paddle with the word WHORE spelled out in cut-out letters, and he was grinning. "This is new—want to give it a try?"

Preston swallowed hard, trying not to think about the way the paddle would leave the word imprinted on his ass. "I'm ah, good, thanks."

"Ace, please—you know how the new ones are. Hey, are you okay? You look a little pale." A smaller, white man with short blond hair and glasses hurried over and motioned to a nearby seat that Preston sank into gratefully. "Now, take a breath and tell us what you need."

"I'm have a bi-crisis," Preston blurted out. "And I lost a bet."

"Ah. Well, sometimes losing is actually winning. My name's Wilder."

"Wilder as in..." Preston motioned toward the front of the building and up toward where the Ace's Wild sign hung.

"Yes, I'm a co-owners, with my partner, Ace, who's not as scary as he pretends to be."

"I'm Preston."

"It's great to meet you." Wilder motioned to the wall. "Does losing the bet include picking something out in this shop?"

"I uh...have a specific list."

"Son, there's nothing you can ask for that'll shock us." Ace leaned in and patted his shoulder, still holding the WHORE paddle.

"Trust him on that." Wilder took the paddle from him. "We've got a lot of compassion for first-timers."

"Second," Preston corrected, wondering why he was spilling his guts to these men. "First with this person."

"And this person—they're special?" Wilder asked.

"He's everything," Preston heard himself say before he pulled his shit together. "I need fur-lined cuffs and an anal hook."

Ace pushed his lips together and nodded approvingly. "Nice choices. Follow me. Any particular color?"

"Pink," he ground out, and he caught Ace's grin.

"Don't knock a punishment, boy. Trust me."

For now, Preston would have to. Because he sure as shit didn't trust himself. He noted that Ace picked out four cuffs, wrist and ankle, and although Jagger hadn't specified that, Preston didn't argue.

When they got to the area with the anal hooks, Preston just stared at the vast array of sizes. Ace didn't hesitate, grabbed one with a silver ball that looked like it wouldn't kill Preston, and handed it to him. "Jagger said you'd be coming in."

Christ, Preston was going to kill Jagger, and his expression must've shown exactly that, because Ace simply smiled. "He just told us to help you out without embarrassing you."

"But there's no stopping Ace from that," Wilder said affectionately as they approached the register. "You were almost in the clear."

Preston sighed and figured there wasn't much these men hadn't been privy to about other people's sex lives over the years. "Yeah, well, I've got everything I need."

"I'd like to suggest a few other items," Ace told him.

"These were the only things on my list."

Ace cocked a brow. "Jagger gave you a list, but there's nothing to say that you can't give him things too. Just because he's into the scene doesn't mean you can't shake him up."

Wilder smiled and Preston found himself being led by both men down several other aisles until he had a collection of toys and other items, including the WHORE paddle, a butt plug, and a spreader bar. And lube.

Preston tried to protest. "I'm not...the first scene..."

"You don't have to use this during your first scene with him. But you should use it. And you'll know exactly when you need to."

"Listen to him," Wilder urged. "He's like a sexual psychic."

Preston watched as the men stared at each other affectionately, embracing openly. Hell, if that's what these toys did, he'd take the entire store.

By the time he'd left, Preston had an open invitation to dinner at their house and two bags full of toys—"One for now and one for later," as Ace had put it.

Preston knew that collecting the toys was the easiest part of what was going to happen tonight.

CHAPTER EIGHT

Jagger

JAGGER HAD BEEN THERE for half an hour, pacing. Muttering to himself. Planning. Praying he didn't fuck this all up.

Thinking of the many ways he could. Those had been running continuously through his head all night. There were times he almost convinced himself that the best thing to do was roll on top of Preston and start kissing the hell out of him. Pin him down in the bed and keep this out of the playroom.

But he knew the playroom was the right place to start this. He was counting on that, and his experience as a Dom—and his experience with Preston—to lead him through this.

He was also wearing the leather pants Preston had seemed so interested in, and he'd stripped his shirt and shoes off.

He'd half expected to be searching out Preston when it got close to nine, but he'd shown, right on time.

That was the biggest step. Jagger could deal with anything from here. He nodded in Preston's direction as Preston stopped in his tracks and stared. Breathed. And stared some more.

Another good sign. And he'd put on worn jeans and a plain black tee, his hair looking like he'd been raking his fingers through it.

It took a lot to make Preston nervous, but tonight, he definitely was.

"Hey," Preston managed uncertainly, holding the bag from Ace's Wild. Two bags, which was...interesting.

As much as Jagger wanted to gather and soothe him, he knew that if he didn't take this step, there would always be unanswered questions between them. Letting either of them off the hook wasn't an option. "Put the bags on the bench, then strip down."

Preston narrowed his eyes but didn't argue, instead doing exactly what he'd been told with the bags before stripping unceremoniously. Jagger took in the muscles, the scars, in a way he hadn't been able to while sleeping next to the man.

No, this was much different. Preston had been naked in front of Jagger before, yes, but somehow not *this* naked. Or this aroused.

"Can we just get this over with?" Preston shifted as Jagger dragged his gaze from the man's cock slowly up to his face.

Oh no. "You'll talk when I say so. This is my time, and all you need to do is follow a goddamned direction."

To his surprise, Preston nodded and waited for Jagger to riffle through the first bag, pulling out the pink cuffs and the anal hook. "Perfect."

He put the hook down and walked toward Preston with the cuffs. Wordlessly, he wrapped them around Preston's wrists and then ankles, checking to make sure they weren't too tight or too loose. He was still on his knees, Preston's dick inches from his face when he glanced up, noting the high flush on his friend's cheeks. "Pink's a good color on you."

"Fuck you."

Jagger smiled and slowly stood, remaining oh so damned close. "You seemed to enjoy the color with Shara. I wanted to give you more of what you wanted."

"Again, fuck you, Jagger." Preston's teeth were clenched, and he jumped when Jagger put a hand on his biceps to lead him over to the leather bench.

"Hands and knees," he instructed, and Preston did as he asked, his erection hanging heavily. Jagger made quick work of securing him, wanting to see him with a ball gag in but knowing he needed to hear Preston's moans.

He left Preston there, helpless, to watch Jagger go through the second bag, trying not to come in his goddamned pants. He took out the butt plug, the spreader bar, and the ball gag. They were all things Jagger already owned, and the significance of Preston offering them to him wasn't lost on either man.

He held up the WHORE paddle. "Interesting choice." He stroked a hand over it, then tapped his palm. Preston probably didn't even realize he'd let out a low moan.

Jagger moved closer, running the paddle down Preston's spine, rubbing it on his ass cheeks. "I prefer using my hands when I'm with someone for the first time. If you need more pain than that, you won't be getting it tonight."

The unspoken part being, "You'll have to ask for another session." Jagger would make sure Preston did.

Preston nodded, like he'd lost the power of speech.

"Red for stop. Yellow to slow down." Again, Preston nodded. Jagger cupped a hand over the back of his neck. "What do you want, Pres? What are you really after?"

"I want to feel," Preston said quietly, his voice barely a whisper. "I want to not be numb anymore."

"I can help with that," Jagger assured him.

"I don't want things to change between us."

"It's too late for that—we both know it. There's no going back. At this point, forward's the only way through it." He wanted to explore the muscled ridges along Preston's back with his teeth and tongue, to bite and soothe and mark his body up, leaving no doubt in Preston's mind as to who'd claimed him. Who he belonged to.

But would Preston understand that Jagger also belonged to him equally as much? Probably not. And that was what Jagger would need to rectify.

Preston

It was nothing like Preston had imagined. No, it was so much better—hotter. More humiliating, which he should hate, but that only added to his need. He was so exposed. Strapped down, held open for his best friend's perusal.

It was Jagger in those leather pants, shirtless, which put his tattoos on full display. Intricate Celtic swirls entwined with crosses and other symbols, all of which meant something to Jagger. They trailed up over his shoulder, down his back and arms, all the way to the backs of his hands.

"How long have you wanted this, Pres?" Jagger's voice was as light as the fingers he ran along Preston's spine, lingering over each inch. "Because I've wanted you—this—for a hell of a long time."

Preston felt his breath quicken, but his throat was tight. His mind raced. Colors raced through his mind. Green.

Green. Greengreengreen.

Jagger let out a low chuckle that went straight up Preston's spine. "Yeah, baby. I'll make it all better tonight."

Do it. Do it now.

"You know why I picked these cuffs?" Jagger continued.

To humiliate me.

"To turn you on, baby." Jagger's hands ran down his back as he answered his own question. "You liked them the other night, and it had nothing to do with Shara."

Fuck, Jagger was right. Preston flexed his fists and wondered how he'd stumbled on a kink.

"You know why you like these? Because I know."

Yes, Preston wanted to know. He nodded, finally managed, "Tell me why."

"No, babe, you're not the one giving the orders." Jagger's voice in and of itself was a turn-on, sliding over Preston's naked body like a warm touch.

Everything narrowed to his touch. Fingertips on skin. Scraping, rubbing, circling. Probing.

Taking.

When one lubed finger entered him, he tensed until Jagger murmured, "Relax. Take it. The only hurt you'll get is the kind you like."

How did he know?

"Because I know you. Watched you. Studied you, and held you while you slept."

As close as lovers...

A groan drummed up in his throat as he let Jagger's finger in—and he was rewarded with a touch that made him buck up and see Heaven.

"And what did we find here?" Jagger asked, amusement in his voice.

Whatever the fuck it was, Shara hadn't unearthed it. Had to have been purposely too, because it wasn't like Jagger had to work that hard to find it.

Which he did, rubbing it over and over again, until Preston heard himself keening.

"Yeah, hit the right spot. It all makes sense now, right?" Jagger murmured.

Jagger added a second finger, and Preston would let him add all of them as long as he kept touching that spot.

He realized he was moving his hips, fucking Jagger's fingers more than Jagger's fingers were fucking him...

"That's it, sweetheart. Show me what you want." With his free hand, Jagger began to spank him, bringing his palm down hard and quick, hitting each ass cheek and making Preston still in surprise. And then Jagger was fucking him with his fingers, spanking him hard until the line between pain and pleasure blurred and everything was just perfect. His mind was free of everything—everything but how good it was, and he heard the cries and groans ripping from his throat at the feel of the man's hands on his bare skin.

He'd craved this.

Wanted Jagger to make him fly apart. And Jagger seemed to want the same thing, because he was crooning and fingering and there were hard smacks...and another and another, until he didn't know which was up.

Until he was flying, his climax washing over him like a goddamned tidal wave. His body convulsed with pleasure as he spurted into Jagger's hand for what seemed like forever.

When his dick stopped pulsing, he drew in a long, ragged breath, screwed his eyes shut, not wanting it to end.

"Taste yourself." Jagger's finger was suddenly in his mouth, and Preston sucked it, making eye contact with his friend. "Keep going. Clean my hand."

Preston did, his cheeks flushed as he licked his own come, cleaning Jagger's hand, filling his mouth with the salty, slightly bitter taste.

Jagger leaned in close, like he was going to give Preston a kiss. Instead, he brought his thumb to his mouth—which still had Preston's come on it—and sucked it.

Which made Preston shudder through a second, unexpected orgasm that caught Jagger by surprise as well.

Good. Fuck you—I can surprise you the way you surprised me.

Everything at the edges of his vision blurred, burned away, to bring his focus squarely on Jagger and Jagger alone.

"I want to pull you over my lap and spank you for running from me. From us," Jagger hissed after several long moments.

"So fucking do it. Punish me." Being put over Jagger's knees, bare-assed, toes digging into the sheets like that would help anything...

"No, not tonight."

But another night. Please. He wanted Jagger to fuck him with more than just his fingers. Wanted Jagger to open him up, split him in two, the way Preston had been dreaming about forever.

Wanted this night not to end. Because Jagger had taken away his choice tonight. But if Preston wanted more? He'd have to ask for it.

Would he be too proud to do so? "What happens now?" Preston asked, his voice hoarse and scratchy. It reminded him of how loud he'd been, and his face got hot.

Jagger cupped a hand under his chin. "What do you want to happen, Pres?"

"I don't want to lose you. Lose what we had."

Jagger gave him a soft smile. "Okay."

"It's hard to think."

"I'd imagine so. Come on—let's get you wiped down and off to bed."

"Alone?"

Jagger helped him up. "You're never alone with me, Pres. You've always known that."

Once he was on the bed, Jagger stood, like he was leaving. "Where are you going?"

Jagger's expression was a cross between grief and anger, but Preston knew him too well. The man was angry at himself. "We can come back from this."

"Really?" Preston half choked out.

"Yes, really. This was intimate. You're vulnerable, but you'd be so much more so in my bed, underneath me—my dick buried in your throat, then in your ass. You're scratching the hell out of my back because you're barely hanging on to me while I take you..."

"Jagger, come on."

Jagger leaned in, a light hand around Preston's throat. Possessive. "It's been a long, slow burn for me. I denied it for as long as I possibly could. I slept around. Contented myself with the fact that we were ride or die. That you'd always be in my life. No matter what, you always will be. But I'm selfish and greedy, Preston, and if I can have all of you, that's what I want. From this point, it's up to you. It always has been."

"Don't...please." His voice caught and Jagger's hand moved away immediately. Preston closed his eyes and woke up what seemed like seconds later, in a towel, on the bed. He'd been wiped down, and Shara was there.

"Hey, Preston. Jagger said you'd be more comfortable with me here," she said quietly.

Preston's gut tightened. He swore he could still feel Jagger's touches even though the man wasn't close enough anymore. "He didn't stay."

Shara shook her head. "I want to tell you he's a prick. And he is. But I also understand why. This is intimate, Pres, and if he can't have all of you...this part might break him."

"He's too strong to break."

"Everyone thinks that...until they fall in love." Shara cradled him. "Relax. I'll wake you in a bit."

"I have—"

"I know, honey." Shara's hand threaded in his hair comfortingly. "If you don't want to go up and get into bed with him, Preston, don't. You might need a night apart. To think. To decide."

But the decision had been made the damned day Jagger had

walked up to him at the high school and claimed him in front of the other boys. This? Was just something he had to accept for himself.

He'd been so driven to prove himself, make something of himself beyond his family and without Jagger's help that he'd probably pushed away feelings he might've realized were there a lot sooner.

But he didn't deal in regrets. Jagger was still here, still wanted him.

Preston was fully ready to give him everything they both wanted.

CHAPTER NINE

Jagger

JAGGER HOVERED OUTSIDE THE DOOR, forcing himself not to go in and carry Preston up to bed. He pressed his forehead to the cool steel door, knowing Preston needed to make this decision for himself. Normal aftercare would involve Preston in his arms, but if Preston didn't want anything more...

Aftercare was the most vulnerable part of this entire experience, in Jagger's opinion. He'd never be able to come back from that, and he wasn't stupid enough to think he could.

Finally, he backed away from the door and waited in the club. Finally, Shara came into the bar area. "Where is he?"

"He went upstairs," she told him, obviously pissed. "I told him he didn't have to."

Jagger nodded.

"I hope you appreciate that I saved his prostate virginity for you," Shara continued.

Jagger rolled his eyes. "I'll get on my knees and do that."

"You should've been there for aftercare, and you know it."

"This is my goddamned club, Shara. Or did you forget that?" he growled.

"If you're in charge of the club—and the dungeons and the Doms? Then you should lead by example." She wasn't scared to stand up to him, and most nights he'd be happy about that.

"You were more than happy to provide Preston's aftercare the other night."

"Is that what this is about?" she demanded. "If I hadn't done that, you two would still be circling each other. Pining away for each other. I did you both a favor. Stop being a dick and take the gift Preston's giving you."

Haughtily, she flung her hair over her shoulder and walked away, her heels clicking on the bare floor...leaving Jagger alone with his guilt and fear.

Finally, when he couldn't stand it any longer, he went upstairs and opened the door to his apartment quietly, half expecting to see Preston on the couch. But no, Preston was in his bed, on his usual side...and the covers were turned down on Jagger's side.

An invitation.

Jagger took it, crawled under the sheets, curled around Preston, and just breathed.

Jagger was up and out of bed early the next morning. Preston was stirring too, but neither of them was ready to deal with what had happened last night.

Or maybe you're just too much of a coward to face facts.

Protecting Preston was getting more difficult with him ready to run at every single turn.

So he went into his office and worked on the books and other distracting tasks until the early afternoon, when Stuart came in with a beer and a sandwich.

Jagger wished it were Preston coming in to interrupt him. To tell him he didn't regret anything that happened. Instead, he took the lunch with a nod.

Instead of leaving, Stuart sat across from him.

"I'm assuming you've got something to say."

Stuart nodded slowly. "What's going on between you and Preston?"

Jagger downed half a beer before he trusted himself to answer, and even then it was a bullshit one. "What do you mean?"

Stuart sighed. "You're fucking now."

"No, we had a scene. A small one. You don't have to fuck to have a scene. How can you work here and not know the difference?"

"With you and Preston, I don't think there is one."

That truth zinged through Jagger. He drained the beer while wishing it was something stronger.

"You're sucking the bottle like it's a dick," Stuart observed, then added innocently, "Maybe use Preston's instead?"

"I'd throw this bottle at you, but I refuse to waste it." Jagger's voice was rough, his cock hard at the thought of sucking Preston's. "I don't know what's going on between us."

"Hadn't noticed." Stuart rolled his eyes. "Want to know what I think?"

"About as much as I want to shove a pencil in my eye."

Stuart ignored that. "I think that you're lovers and neither of you realize it."

"That's ridiculous."

"The lovers part—or the not realizing it part?"

"Both."

Jagger shot Stuart the finger, even as he considered the man's words. What did Preston think was happening? He'd scheduled time with Shara in order to make Jagger...mad? Jealous? A combination of the two?

Of course, Jagger had immediately penciled himself in over Shara, and she hadn't complained. Preston wouldn't be surprised to see him tonight...but Jagger could make sure that wasn't the only thing he wasn't surprised at.

You couldn't even provide aftercare without getting too attached to the idea of being with Preston. "I'm trying not to freak him out."

"He looks freaked-out to me." Stuart shook his head. "So you two hooked up and decided not to talk about it?"

Jagger shrugged. "Talking's overrated."

"You sure you can trust him?"

"Don't start with me on this again, Stuart. You know I do."

"But Preston wasn't born into this life."

"One more word, Stuart," Jagger began, when the now all-too-familiar Private Number showed on his screen. Because the real threat was on the other end of this number, and Stuart needed to remember that.

Preston

Jagger had been out of bed by the time Preston woke that morning. Which was good, because it completely avoided any awkwardness... but it also pissed him off.

He wasn't sure what he'd expected, but it hadn't been aftercare from Shara. And even though he understood Jagger's hesitance, he resented the fact that the ball was always in his court.

Because you're the one who always leaves.

By the time he went downstairs to work on the security system,

Jagger was locked in his office and Stuart was out doing whatever it was Stuart did. Preston got to work, until he needed to run out to the hardware store to pick up a few things. By that time, Stuart was back.

"I'm running down the block. I'm setting the alarm. Don't open the door for anyone."

"Got it," Stuart said with an eye roll.

"We're not expecting any deliveries. No one comes in until I'm back."

"I don't know how we've survived this long without you."

Preston growled under his breath, texted Jagger about the alarm, and walked out the side door. His situational awareness was always on high alert, but the Army had trained it into a personality trait. He scanned the area constantly, delineating everyone and everything he saw by threat level.

The only thing to distract him was his sore ass, a constant reminder of what he'd surrendered to last night. He rambled through the hardware store, grabbing the wire and other essentials, anxious to get back. Until Preston got a handle on what exactly was happening with Jagger, the club, and the threats, he wouldn't be comfortable having Jagger out of his sight.

Of course, having Jagger in his sight now was also as uncomfortable as hell.

Speaking of hell, Preston noticed that a dark SUV had pulled up outside of the hardware store. Leaning against it, waiting, was Agent Saunders.

He noted that the man behind the counter was now staring at him as he handed Preston his purchases.

Preston had seen agents work like this in the past—give store-owners his picture in return for cash if they called in when they saw him. So this fucker had probably been paid as well, judging by the look of fear on his face. Then again, it wasn't like Saunders didn't know where Preston was staying.

"Thanks for everything," he said pleasantly to the man behind the counter and walked out smiling and calm. He glanced at Saunders and pretended to be shocked. "Agent Saunders, what a surprise. I guess you're really enjoying North Carolina. Boston must be boring in comparison."

"I'm following the action."

Preston stared at the man who'd been following him for years. "And here I am, trying to avoid it."

"You are the action, Preston."

"I'm flattered, Saunders." Preston batted his lashes at him. "But I'm taken."

Until he'd spoken the words out loud, he didn't know how badly he'd wanted that to be true.

"By Jagger? Because if you weren't working for him before, you are now," Saunders pointed out.

"I'm helping out an old friend until I decide what I want to be when I grow up." Preston began to walk, passing Pet World, and making a mental note to talk to Jagger about adopting a dog. Or two.

Saunders fell into step beside him. "Your parents are very worried about you, Preston. And they should be, with the company you keep."

"I can just imagine how that visit went. My parents are great hosts, as long as you do exactly what they say." Preston kept his voice as neutral as possible. "Sounds like you're falling into step with them."

Saunders moved quickly into his personal space, stopping him. "It's more than concern, you little asshole. I know you think you can handle this, but you need to understand that I'm committed to bringing your friend down. I don't care if you're caught in the crossfire, but your parents do. So I'm giving you another chance to tell me what you know about Jagger King."

"He's great with a paddle and handcuffs. And he's bi," Preston offered with a smile.

"Are you?"

Preston laughed. "You interested in a session with him, Saunders? I'm betting he can get rid of some of that tension you're holding on to."

He pushed past and Saunders didn't follow him farther. When he reentered the club, Stuart was nowhere to be found, but Jagger was waiting for him, much like Saunders had been.

"Hey," Preston called over his shoulder as he rearmed the alarm. "I'll have the mess out of here by the time you open."

"Okay. I'm not worried about that though."

"What are you worried about?" Preston asked as Jagger moved to close the gap between them. There was a delicate dance happening between them, and both men were about as subtle as a Claymore mine and in need of the same explicit instructions.

"You." Jagger's dark eyes bored through his. "Always you."

"Listen...before I left, I replaced Shara's name on the booking. With yours." He rubbed the pulse point on his neck, felt it jumping wildly under his fingertips. Jagger's eyes followed the motion. "Nine tonight."

"Sure that's what you want?" Jagger asked, his eyes narrowed.

I want you to look at me the way you did last night. The way you did after we kissed.

But instead of saying any of that, he simply nodded.

"Nine it is, then," Jagger murmured under his breath, and all Preston could do was watch Jagger saunter away.

CHAPTER TEN

Jagger

JAGGER HAD to force himself not check the time nine thousand times, but finally it was nine. He headed casually toward the blue room, walked in, and found it empty.

Preston wasn't there. His gut tightened and he was about to slam the door shut when he saw the note on the bench.

> J—
> *I'm upstairs. In your bed. Naked. If you're interested, that's where I want to play tonight.*
> *-P*

Jagger had to stop himself from taking the stairs two at a time. *If you're interested...*

He forced himself to walk into his apartment slowly, heart thudding. By the time he turned the corner into his bedroom, he was rock hard.

"About time." Preston was lying in bed, his lower body barely covered by the sheet.

"Lose the sheet," Jagger told him. "My bed, my rules."

Preston smirked. "Still have that need for total control?"

"With you? Yes." Jagger moved forward, hearing the low growl in his words. He was pleased to see that Preston had brought the toys from the other day with him...and the pink cuffs were already circling his wrists and ankles. "What does this mean? Is this a session, or is this us?"

Preston was kneeling on the mattress so they were chest to chest. "It's both. It's us. It's everything."

It was easy for Jagger to forget how goddamned new Preston was to all of this. He'd been surrounded by it thanks to Jagger, but before last night, Preston had only been with women.

"Last night was perfect. But I want more."

"More what?"

"More of you. Us. This." Preston moved closer, his hands sliding up Jagger's shirt. Exploring. And Jagger let him. "I'm confident in the field. In my job. But with this, with you...if you're not okay with this..."

"You didn't want talking. You wanted to be tied down, remember? You can't get enough of it," Jagger reminded him, his voice husky, his dick jutting between them.

Preston lunged forward and grabbed his face and kissed him hard. Jagger allowed him to start it, but by the end, he was holding Preston's jaw, punishing his mouth with deep, tongue-fucking kisses until Preston was a whimpering, slobbering, groveling mess.

"Please, Jagger. I need it."

"Explicit."

"Need you to tie me down and spank me. Finger me." He paused. "I need you to fuck me after you open me up with your fingers."

"Fingers aren't enough anymore?" Jagger asked, and Preston shook his head. "You want a dildo?"

Preston's hand moved between Jagger's legs. "No. You." Jagger nodded and ran a finger over the pink cuffs, enjoying how Preston blushed. "I'm way too fucking attached to these things," he muttered.

"It's a mild kink," Jagger assured him as he smoothed the hair from Preston's forehead. "You wanted me, Pres. And you've made me wait a long damned time. You're not getting away with that anymore."

Preston shuddered.

Jagger noticed, murmured, "Pretty baby," as his fingers played with one of Preston's nipples, working it. Making Preston stand sharply at attention. "Baby wants me sucking his pretty tits."

"Please. Yes." Jagger's mouth lowered to suck on his left nipple, and fuck, Preston's cock jumped in response. He grabbed for Jagger's shoulders, wanting to rut against him as his cock leaked as Jagger's tongue licked roughly before taking the taut nub between his teeth. Preston's entire body jerked. "Jagger...dammit."

Jagger tortured him for several more minutes, holding his hips so he was unable to get any friction, suckling his nipples until they were red and swollen and hot. Only then did he pull back.

"Hands and knees, baby." When Preston did as he asked, Jagger moved in to connect the wrist and ankle restraints together, which left Preston open and vulnerable. Exactly the way Jagger wanted him. "You've been thinking about this all day, haven't you? Been planning our session?"

He smacked Preston's ass cheeks lightly, and Preston hissed at the hits. His ass was still slightly pink from the night before, and Jagger admired it for a few moments before rustling in the Ace's Wild bag.

He took out the WHORE paddle, leaned forward, and held it in front of Preston's face. "Kiss it for me, baby."

Preston closed his eyes and brought his lips to the leather paddle.

Preston

Was this really happening? Preston had kissed the WHORE paddle, and now, Jagger had it poised, resting on his ass. Rubbing it there as a tease while asking, "You want this? Chose it special for me?"

Preston could only nod, but Jagger didn't make him answer. Not with words. But once the two hard slaps hit him, Preston cried out, "Jagger!" and lurched forward. His eyes teared.

It was less about the pain and more the burning fucking need. The fact that he'd be branded with the word he suddenly didn't mind.

Jagger's whore.

"Fuck—looks good, Pres." Jagger ran a soothing hand over his ass, pulled the cheeks apart...and then he buried his face in Preston's ass.

"Jagger...please...you can't..." Preston's words became garbled, incoherent cries. "This isn't..."

"You're safe with me, baby."

After several moments, Preston's cries of *Jagger* and *god* and *please* and *more* were harsh and throaty. His cheeks flushed hot at how completely vulnerable he was, again. How Jagger could do something this intimate. But want and need quickly overrode that, especially when Jagger tongued his rim. And then he rubbed the scruff of his beard hard against the sensitive area.

Preston squirmed...and pushed his ass back against Jagger, wanting more.

Jagger gave it to him.

"Fuck...your beard." Preston panted.

"Why do you think I grew it?" Jagger rubbed it in between the sensitive area between Preston's cheeks, making sure to rub the rough over the man's hole. He obviously wanted Preston to feel it—now, and for days to come. He buried his face in Preston's ass, sucking on his hole. Preston jumped—or tried to, but he was too tightly bound to move.

Instead, he began to beg. Plead. Use Jagger's name like a chant.

"Please. Please." He didn't know what he was begging for, but he trusted that Jagger did. Pressed his forehead to the bed as Jagger's arm circled around him and dragged his mouth up Preston's spine, licking, nipping, soothing, and not gently. But not dominating him.

No, Jagger was seducing him. Inviting him to continue. Preston's groan was enough for Jagger to lean up and murmur *good* and *baby* and *love this* in his ear, even as his lubed fingers began to enter Preston's ass. One, then two, and fuck, it burned, but once Jagger's finger hit his gland, Preston was begging for more.

"Ready, baby?" Jagger's breath was warm on his cheek, and yes, Preston felt like he'd been ready forever. Finally, he heard the rip of a condom wrapper and felt Jagger's cock slide in between his ass cheeks, teasing him. But he only did that for a few moments before he was entering Preston, telling him to breathe, to push out, to take him in.

Preston's forehead pressed the mattress, his entire body breaking out in chills. He was slick with sweat, and his mind was dealing with that thin line between pleasure and pain.

Finally, Jagger was inside of him, pressing his prostate. Moving, rocking, and everything was white light and perfect. Jagger palmed his cock and stroked it as he took Preston, riding him until they both came, Preston first and Jagger right behind him.

Jagger rolled off him, unhooked the restraints, and helped massage Preston's limbs to get the circulation going. But Preston felt boneless, just let Jagger handle him while he lay belly down on the bed. His ass was sore, throbbed, and he was the happiest he'd been in a hell of a long time.

Jagger leaned in and murmured, "You're always fighting, Pres—for as long as I've known you. At this point, it's habit. And I've seen you use it—but never with me. Never...until now."

Fuck. He hated how right Jagger was. "It's been a lot..."

Jagger's hand slid through his hair. "I know, baby. I know you've been through shit and you're going through more shit, and I want to be there. I hate watching you flail."

"You can't always help me."

"Why not?"

"I'm not weak, Jagger. I'm not." His voice nearly broke on the last word.

"Is that what you...fuck, you believe I think you're weak?"

"I'm weak for you."

Jagger's face broke open, that look that Preston craved came across his face. "That's not weakness, baby. That's something you don't want to admit to yourself." Jagger dragged a finger across Preston's bottom lip. "You don't think I'm a pushover for you?"

"You weren't the one strapped down."

"Do you know how strong you have to be to give in to your needs— to submit? Do you know you run the show? I follow your lead." Preston frowned, and Jagger sighed. "All these years you've been hanging out with me and you don't know that?"

"Purposeful avoidance?" Preston mumbled, and Jagger snorted.

Jagger's eyes darkened with desire. "No more avoiding."

Preston bent his head and leaned his forehead down on Jagger's shoulder. Jagger's hand immediately went to the back of Preston's neck, gently but heavy. Claiming. "I can't..."

"You won't," Jagger corrected with a tenderness that made Preston's heart beat faster, and when the hell had he gotten so soft?

Did it matter? Jagger didn't seem to think so. "I'm so fucked-up."

"There's very few who aren't, baby." Jagger propped up on his elbow. Preston still kept his face half-buried in the pillow. "Are we ever going to talk about this? What started it all?" Jagger demanded.

"Christ, can't a guy enjoy his afterglow?" Preston grumbled.

"*You* kissed *me*."

"I know." Preston tilted his head and stared up at his friend. "I was confused."

"Are you still?"

"No. Just a little scared. Off my game," he admitted.

"I can work with that. Let's not talk about it tonight. Tomorrow, we'll put cards on the table, but tonight..." Jagger tugged him closer. "I'm not done with you."

"Jesus, you fucking ruin me, Jagger. You goddamned wreck me."

Jagger leaned in. "I'll take that as a compliment. And I do it because you deserve it. And I mean that in the best way possible."

Preston tried to keep his head buried in the pillow, until Jagger wound a hand in his hair and forced Preston's eyes to his. And that's when Preston got lost.

Jagger's eyes were always so pretty. The rest of him was hard and messy and dirty, all big and masculine, leather boots and facial hair, but his eyes were light blue with green and gold flecks...like endless sunshine. "Your eyes," he managed.

"I'm not dealing with your flattery bullshit."

"Shut up." His voice sounded slurred, like he'd been drinking tequila, and he barely had any control over his limbs. He was boneless. Sweating. Content and oddly needy at the same time, and Jagger seemed to know that. Alternately held and stroked him as he came down.

"Beauty and the beast," Jagger murmured finally.

"You've never been a beast."

Jagger had a strong, interesting face. Wide cheekbones and forehead and the majority of his back and chest and arms were covered in tattoos by the time he was twenty. He looked like a thug, and he'd never minded that. It'd gotten him where he'd needed to go—and he'd never wanted for company.

He'd never much cared about who it was, as long as his family—and Preston—were close by. "So what am I?"

"Just mine, Jagger. All fucking mine."

CHAPTER ELEVEN

Preston

PRESTON WOKE to Jagger's kiss on the back of his neck. Sunlight streamed in through the windows, and that's when Preston realized that Jagger hadn't gone back down to the club at all last night.

"You stayed here the whole time?" he asked now.

"Mmmhmmm," Jagger hummed into his shoulder. "Problem?"

"Didn't you have…"

"Regulars? I already spoke with them to let them know they'd have to find a new Dom here." Jagger's fingers grazed his stomach and trailed down to his cock. "I'm hoping there was a good reason for it."

"Fuck," Preston breathed out when Jagger's palm closed around his cock and stroked. He leaned in and bit Jagger's shoulder, let his hand run down Jagger's hip, finding Jagger's cock and fisting it.

Jagger stilled when Preston began to stroke him. Preston glanced up to find the man staring at him, and only then did Jagger resume his rhythm. Together, they jerked each other off, slowly. Preston enjoyed watching Jagger's mouth drop open, hearing his breathing quicken even though he was way more out of control than Jagger was.

"Pres, s'good," Jagger murmured. "No idea how long I've pictured this."

"Tell me," Preston urged. "Did you want to do this to me when you watched me do homework."

"Wanted to make you do your homework with me sucking your dick. Wanted to bend you over and make you to suck mine when you made me read."

Preston laughed. "If I'd known that would've helped..." Jagger groaned as Preston's hand spread up, the soft velvet skin encasing the steel rod firmly in his hand. He used his thumb to circle the tip around the head of Jagger's cock, just like Preston liked to do to himself when he jerked off. "I like making you lose control."

"Only for you." Jagger leaned in and kissed him, hard and fast, crushing their mouths together as he came, all over Preston's hand, coating their bellies. Preston followed almost immediately, mainly because of the sounds Jagger made when his orgasm hit.

Jagger banded an arm around him, pulling them together, making more of a mess. Preston nuzzled his neck, wondering how he'd managed to miss all of this for so damned long.

"Shower?" Jagger asked finally, just as his phone began to ring. He frowned and glanced at it. "What's up, Stuart? Yeah? No, I'll come down now." He put the phone down. "Delivery issue. Stuart said I should be there for it. I'll be back up soon."

He went to the bathroom and came back wiping his stomach with a wet washcloth. He'd brought one for Preston as well, and Preston cleaned himself while watching Jagger slide on a pair of jeans and a sweatshirt, covering up the ink that should never, ever be covered up.

"You're eye-fucking me," Jagger called to him on the way out. He glanced over his shoulder and gave Preston a crooked smile, his eyes soft, before he left. Preston lay back on the pillows, smelling their mingling scents in the sheets and on him, and thought about how showering was overrated. He stretched, thought about turning over and going back to sleep for a few minutes...

But Jagger didn't really deal with deliveries, so Stuart calling for him specifically meant there was an issue. If his brain wasn't so sex-fogged, he might've caught that sooner, but now it got him dressed and down the stairs in bare feet. Thankfully, Jagger seemed fine, standing outside with the driver of the truck, going through a clipboard of paperwork.

"Coming down to save the day?" Stuart's voice came up from behind him. Preston stilled, then turned and found Stuart sneering at him. "Don't worry—I can take care of him just as well as you. Better than, actually."

"You always say that, Stu. And he still wants me here, running his security. Working with him. Why's that?"

"You really think this is going to work out between you and Jagger? That you're going to sail into the sunshine together? Bullshit. You'll run again. You always run, and I stay behind and pick up the pieces."

Preston stared at Stuart's throat, taking great pleasure in picturing his hand wrapped around it. "You obviously wanted this moment alone with me. So lay it all out, because I've been around for fourteen years and I'm not going anywhere."

"Did he tell you that the threats are because of you?" Stuart demanded.

"What?"

"No, of course he wouldn't. Always protecting you."

Preston couldn't argue with that. He'd assumed that Jagger was being purposely vague about the threats so Preston wouldn't have to lie to the police. Also, because he was still technically could be called to active duty at any moment. "Jagger knows my family's trying to fuck things up. It's why I stayed away."

"But now you're back. And it's no coincidence that the threats have started up." Stuart spoke the truth—Preston knew that. "You're ruining him. You'll be the one to take him down, and the ironic thing is, he'll still forgive you. You know he's going legit. Giving up the family business—for you. Protecting Preston again."

"What does that have to do with the threats?"

"The King family runs things a certain way—the last vestige of civilization in a wild west. People aren't happy. And law enforcement sees this as their opportunity to take one last shot at them."

"I didn't ask him to do it."

"He's doing it to keep your family from hurting you. You know your family's got it out for him."

"Because they want me under their thumb."

"You keep thinking that," Stuart muttered. "He always wants to goddamned protect you, and it's coming back to bite him in the ass."

"What aren't you telling me?"

"It's not my place to upset poor Preston." Stuart spat his name. "Doesn't the Army still need you? You can't do nearly as much harm there as you can to Jagger. So if you care anything about him at all, you'll leave. Make the visits few and far between, or else we're going to have a problem."

"Then I guess we're going to have a problem."

"You definitely will."

"Is that a threat, Stuart?"

Stuart's angry expression answered his question. He jerked his chin toward the office. "Jagger's looking at some interesting pictures right now. Hope you've got your story straight."

Before Preston could say anything—or punch Stuart out, which was the better option—Jagger was heading toward them. "Step away, Stuart."

"You're going to let him get away with this?" Stuart asked. When Jagger leveled him with a gaze, Stuart shook his head. "His dick's been poisoning you before you ever touched it."

"Go!" Jagger roared, and Stuart took several steps back before turning on his heel and leaving.

Preston watched Jagger as he stared after Stuart before finally turning his gaze, his eyes still dark with anger.

He handed the envelope he'd been holding out to Preston. "Stuart's been having you followed."

Preston fought a growl and nearly tore the envelope to get to the pictures. They were black and whites from his trip to the hardware store and, of course, showed him getting up close and personal with Saunders. "This is that FBI agent I told you about."

"You didn't mention you saw him the other day."

"I was distracted—it was the day after the blue room. And it was the same old bullshit. He's in my parents' pocket. I gave him some food for thought—that's all."

"Apparently, someone from my camp has been talking to this Agent Saunders very recently. Telling him about my business. Why I moved from Boston."

"And you didn't stop to think it might be Stuart? Or that Stuart might be lying, because he doesn't want me here?" Preston asked calmly.

Jagger glanced at the pictures. "Go to the last one."

Preston did so until he got to the photo of an opened file—there was a piece of paper with his name and information on it. "What the hell is this?"

"Stuart has a source at the local PD who says that there's a CI file that was recently opened...on you."

"I'm a confidential informant for a police department I've never met? Come on, Jagger."

But Jagger's gaze was...odd. He wasn't angry. More like resigned. And his voice was flat when he said, "I think you have to leave."

"Leave? You can't honestly believe—"

Jagger was touching his own face under his eye, mirroring the scar on Preston's cheek. *Ride or die.* "You need to go."

"Fine. Fuck you—I'm out." Preston yanked Jagger's hand off him and walked away.

Whatever—whoever—they were playing this game for, he was going to make it the performance of his goddamned life.

His head spun. What had he missed? He was supposed to be watching out for Jagger, and instead, Preston had somehow let both Stuart and Saunders get the best of him.

Not for goddamned long.

He stuffed the rest of his clothes into his duffle, shouldered it, and walked down the back stairs without running into anyone. He didn't pause when he hit the door, pushed it open, and exited before he turned back and found Stuart and did something he'd really regret.

He'd somehow turned off the soldier part of him when he'd needed it the most. Now, his instincts were screaming, threatening to pull him in different directions.

Instead, he leaned against the brick wall where he'd first kissed Jagger and just breathed. He'd been Jagger's for so long, and then he'd been the Army's, and now?

You're you. Finally.

He could fucking handle anything. So he pushed off the wall and wasn't surprised to find Agent Saunders waiting for him at the end of the block.

"Can I give you a lift home?" Saunders asked.

Preston moved in close—too close, but he was playing his part. Pissing the agent off. He knew it as surely as he knew Jagger still trusted him. "You can fuck off though."

Saunders tsk'd. "I see you're moving out. Sorry things didn't go as planned."

"Things can change."

"He's never going to trust you again. And you never should've trusted him in the first place, Preston. Time to be smart."

"You've been smart enough for both of us, haven't you?" Preston leaned in, but Saunders held his ground. "You've been a busy boy. I think you'd better watch your back."

"Are you threatening me?"

"Just friendly talk." Preston backed away and started walking. "Don't come near me again."

"He'll never believe you, Preston. Not with the CI file."

That bothered Preston more than anything. The fact that Jagger would even go there, think that Preston would—or could—betray him, after all this time? That broke his goddamned heart.

So what are you going to do about it? "What do you plan on doing, Saunders?"

"I'm taking you in for questioning. I'm hoping you'll cooperate— it's for your own good."

It's for your own good, son.

Preston stilled. This was all too fucking familiar.

Ride or die.

Jagger was trying to tell him something—something important.

Had Jagger known this would happen? Did he realize how far everyone involved would go?

You trust him with your life. Keep trusting.

Saunders questioned him for hours. Left him alone in a room with music blasting and no food or water or bathroom breaks, but he'd have to go a hell of a lot harder than this to make a dent in Preston.

Finally, Saunders tried the "I understand you" routine by handing him a cup of coffee, a donut, and the all-too-familiar "I was in the Army too."

Whether it was true or not didn't matter. Preston downed the coffee and the donut before answering. "Couldn't hack it though? It's much easier to follow people around the mean streets of North Carolina, right?"

Saunders frowned.

"Is this really what you want to spend your life doing? I can't believe the FBI doesn't have better things to do. Or maybe you like being a pocket pet for wealthy people."

Saunders slammed his fists on the table "You're Jagger's pocket pet —have been since high school."

"You think you're not close to criminals? Think again. Maybe investigate the people behind this whole mess, and then we'll chat again. Because this has nothing to do with high school. And everything to do with how you're being used."

Saunders left him alone for a long while. It had to be close to midnight when he came back, and suddenly, Preston was free to go.

He walked out of the police station and headed back down toward the warehouse district on foot, wanting to be close enough to Jagger without going back to the club.

Maybe he should've grabbed a cab, but this déjà vu was necessary. Pushed him forward until he turned down an alley cut through two buildings away from the club, and a short walk to the nearest hotel beyond that.

He came up on shadowy figures up ahead.

He kept going until Stuart walked across his path. He was with six men, and one of them was Trumble.

"Just like old times, Preston." Trumble smiled. The years hadn't been kind to him—he looked like he'd taken a pipe across the nose repeatedly. But he was still big.

Big and dumb. Because it was far fucking from old times. Preston might not have had the skills to fight off six men back then, but he sure as hell did now. "I guess you're finally getting what you've always wanted—me gone." He directed his first comment at Trumble, then stared directly at Stuart. "You didn't have the guts to show up yourself that night, did you?"

"I tried to let you leave last time with your goddamned life. Who the hell takes a beating like you did and still sticks around?" Stuart shook his head. "Poor little rich boy who can't take a fucking hint."

"Does Saunders know you're going to kill me? I'm sure my parents won't be happy about that. Then again, maybe this is part of their plan."

Stuart smiled. "Who do you think gave me the idea about all of this in the first place?"

Preston felt the chill run through him. "They put you up to that? Back in high school?"

"They had help with the police department, but yeah, they called me specifically. Paid me too." Stuart shrugged. "Paid me again this time too. You're just too much goddamned trouble, Preston."

"Always have been, I guess." Preston shrugged, his body loose and ready for the fight. Needing it, actually. "I just don't get why any of this really fucking bothers you. You have your place with the Kings."

"That's right—I do, and my father before me did. And we'd have gotten further if it wasn't for your family."

Preston shook his head. "That's a stretch."

"You really don't know. Jagger never told his pretty boy any of it. The son of a bastard? His mother was your father's first wife...before she ran to Sean King."

Preston's mouth opened, then closed. "That can't be true."

"But it is. Sean rescued her. Protected her, just like Jagger protected you. And he pushed my father out because there was only room for Maggie King in his life. I had a shot at finding my place next to Jagger. Helping him bring his business even further along. And then he fucking rescued you like another goddamned stray dog."

Was that true? Did Jagger know who he was from the first?

Did it really fucking even matter? His anger rose to the surface, building to a nearly uncontrollable level. He was a trained soldier, special forces, and fighting with civilians was supposed to be out of the question.

But self-defense? That was allowed. Especially as the six men advanced on him. "You think you've won."

"I know I have. Jagger thinks you're a CI. He wants you gone.

Your parents want you gone, and so do I. There's no one who wants you around anymore, pretty boy."

"I do."

Stuart swiveled around at the sound of Doctor's voice. Doctor stood maybe ten feet behind him and his men. And next to him? Diego. Arthur. Trick and Skully.

And then Jagger walked around the corner. "Hey, Stuart."

Preston almost felt sorry for Stuart. The man turned an unnatural shade of pale but managed to say, "It's not what it looks like."

Jagger didn't bother answering, instead walked up to Preston and stood shoulder to shoulder with him, just like that first day all over again.

"I should've told you everything. I should've been there the first time," Jagger told him. "I hope this makes up for that, just a little."

"More than," Preston told him. "But I can take care of them by myself."

"I know. I want to watch." Jagger smiled, his eyes bright. "You know which one to save for me."

CHAPTER TWELVE

Jagger

JAGGER HAD WATCHED Preston take down Trumble and the other five men who'd attacked him way back when, and this time, there was no contest. Preston held back—a hell of a lot—but it was still sexy as fuck to watch him fight.

Now, those men were on the ground, hands zip-tied behind their backs.

Preston took down the six men, but he'd left Stuart for Jagger. And when the dust had settled and the police arrived, Arthur had acted as their attorney and handed over the recording. It was all the police needed to take Stuart and the rest into custody.

Jagger was relatively sure Agent Saunders would follow—and, at the very least, he'd be leaving Preston alone. The VanValens would be questioned and no doubt buy themselves out of trouble again.

It didn't matter. This was done.

Preston could kill men with his bare hands, was a highly trained, elite soldier...and Jagger had already entrusted his life to him long before any of that.

They were evenly matched in so many ways. Both fighters. Both fiercely protective of what was theirs.

"Are you sure you're all right?" Jagger asked Preston now, and for the millionth time. He was holding ice packs to the man's cheek and ribs, babying the hell out of him, and for once, Preston wasn't saying shit about it, except, "I'm fine because you're here."

Having Stuart tell Preston about Maggie King's connection to the VanValen family hadn't been ideal...but it was going to come out today, no matter what. He held his own ice pack to his cheek where Stuart had sucker punched him. It was the only punch the man had gotten in. "I should've told you about Maggie sooner."

"I guess we were both holding on to some secrets," Preston murmured. He reached out to touch Jagger's raw knuckles. "We need to clean and bandage these."

"We will. But now...talk to me, Pres. Tell me exactly what's going on inside that mind of yours."

"I will. But first..." Preston's hands went to either side of his face, gently, pulled him in and kissed him—a soft, undemanding kiss that quickly turned intense. Jagger let it, let Preston own him in those moments, in a way he'd never let anyone do before. "Think the talking can wait a little bit?"

"Yeah, definitely." Jagger narrowed his eyes at the way Preston was staring at him, and for the first time in probably forever, he felt like prey. And his dick? Seemed to like it. "What do you want, Pres?"

Preston's pretty-boy smile was wicked. "Take out that big, beautiful cock and let me see you palm it."

Jagger smirked and did what was asked of him, because it was easier.

"Run your thumb over the head and swipe that precome—then lick it off your thumb."

Jagger ran his thumb to swipe the pearl of fluid and licked it off slowly, holding Preston's gaze and fuck, this was hot. Preston gave orders well. Maybe next time, he'd ask him to wear his uniform.

"Yeah, baby, you're better at following directions than I thought. Think you can get off on it?"

Jagger let out a harsh pant. "When the fuck did you get so good at this?"

"I might be new to fucking a guy, but I'm not new to restraints. Or being in charge."

"I think I created a monster."

"And way more quickly than you considered." Preston looked smug as he considered Jagger, pants open and riding his hips. "I like you like this. Are you going to let me fuck you?" Preston leaned forward and licked a stripe along Jagger's collarbone, then sucked hard, leaving a mark. He didn't wait for an answer before he was stripping Jagger's shirt off, running his fingers all along the gorgeous ink. "So fucking beautiful."

Jagger shuddered as he let Preston uncover him. The man was kissing and nipping and touching everywhere, exploring every inch of skin he uncovered even as he forced Jagger onto his back. When he was finally naked, Preston hovered over him, still fully dressed.

As Jagger watched, Preston kissed a line down his stomach to his cock.

"You're right—I do crave it," he murmured before taking it into his mouth, causing Jagger to arch off the bed.

"Fucking overachiever," Jagger bit out, and Preston hummed around his cock. What he lacked in finesse he more than made up for in enthusiasm, and soon, Jagger was begging for him to stop. "I want to come with you inside me."

Preston let Jagger's thick length out of his mouth for a second. "Then you can come twice." He sucked Jagger back into his mouth, swirling his tongue around the broad head of Jagger's cock. And he kept his gaze locked on Jagger's.

The sight of Preston's lips stretched around his cock pushed him over the goddamned edge. He grabbed Preston's hair and kept him there. Preston didn't fight at all, instead swallowed what he could and finished, come on his lower lip.

He licked it off and smiled. "I've got a lot of lost time to make up for."

Jagger closed his eyes and tried to recover from the climax that had ripped through him, but Preston wasn't content to let him rest. Instead, there was lube. Fingers, opening him. Jagger played with toys often enough—it was hard to Dom if you didn't know what being a bottom felt like, but to have Preston inside of him?

A jerk-off fantasy come to life. Preston liked pink cuffs. Jagger liked Preston's cock. Preston's everything.

"I want to watch your face," Preston told him as he knelt again between Jagger's legs and ripped open a condom. "We're getting rid of these things fast."

He put a hand on Jagger's hip, another on his shoulder, and then Preston pushed inside steadily, not stopping. Soon enough, both men were breathing harshly, with Jagger willing to accept the pain to find the pleasure.

"You're so goddamned tight, Jag. Does it always feel like this?"

Jagger huffed out a breath. "If you're doing it right."

"Am I?"

"I don't want you to stop, baby. Come on—fuck me hard."

Preston did, pounded him while he wrapped himself around Preston and let himself get taken for the ride of his life.

Lying on the bed in the half-light coming through the window, Jagger turned to face him. "I wanted to tell you myself."

Preston wrapped an arm around Jagger. "I get why you didn't. What does it help? My father's a hateful fuck—that just proves he always was."

"I didn't protect you because of who you were—you have to know that. I didn't even know you were coming to the school. It was only once I heard them say your last name that first day that I knew. But fuck, I figured your family would make things worse for you if I told you any of it." Jagger put a hand over Preston's heart. "All I knew for sure was that Maggie brought you to me. That she would've loved you."

"That means more than you know." Preston shifted.

"The men in my family fall fast and hard. And I know all of this was easier for me." Jagger had accepted his bisexuality from an early age, and hadn't really given a shit about those who didn't understand it. "I knew you needed time, and I tried to be patient."

Preston snorted at that. "You understand that I had to come to you as an equal—whether it was as a friend...or more. I had to make my own way. You get that, don't you?"

Jagger's hand went to the scar, his thumb rubbing it. "I do. But you always made your own way, Pres. You need to know that."

Preston gave him a tense smile. "I'm a liability to you. I always was."

"What are you talking about? Your parents?" Jagger asked, and Preston nodded. "Cards on the table."

Preston took a deep breath and started. "It wasn't ever running from you. It wasn't about that. It was always about you. Protecting you."

"You don't think I'm holding on to guilt for what happened to you? That my family—my father—doesn't?" His voice was tight with emotion. "We're the reason your father went in for you so hard. We're the reason for his vendetta."

"How did Maggie meet your dad?"

"She was forced into the marriage to your dad by her family. They were wealthy. Controlling." Jagger's eyes met his. "When my father first saw her, she'd been trying to steal his car. She was trying to run away. She'd been beaten by her new husband. They'd been married for two weeks."

"Your dad saved her."

"Saved her. Protected her. Said he fell in love with her the second he saw her. Mom said it was mutual." Jagger managed a small smile at the memory. "She was officially protected by the Kings. Back then, it meant that she fell under mob protection too, by default. Her husband —her family—couldn't touch her. But they made her life miserable. She was refused a divorce, so she couldn't remarry."

Which was why people called Maggie King a sinner. Why they called Jagger a bastard.

"It never mattered to my father—in his eyes, they were together forever. It wasn't until after she died that I realized how bad her first husband really was. How much of a vendetta he held against our family. It must've killed him to realize that his plan to send you to public school, to teach you a lesson, backfired so badly." Jagger shook his head, the old anger forcing its way back. He pushed it down to focus on Preston. "He didn't expect that we'd become friends. He figured you'd run from my world. And I didn't want to hurt you. Or force you away. You already felt guilty. And I didn't want to lose you to that goddamned family. Even before I knew the connection, I knew that much was true."

So did Preston. "I knew it. I just didn't recognize it for what it was. I was never attracted to a guy...not until you." His voice was a raw whisper.

"Can't help who you fall for. Why fight it? And don't give me the police and your parents bullshit, because I'm not worried about that. If it's your pride? Get over that too. You're a hero. You served your country. And you lent me money before you left."

"So pay it back, asshole."

Preston

Preston let that hang in the air between them for a long moment before he laughed and Jagger rolled his eyes. He'd never understood why Jagger needed the money, but he hadn't hesitated to give it to him.

Jagger pulled away for a second, opened a drawer in the night table, and presented Preston with what looked like a contract. "Here you go."

"What's this?" It looked like a deed to the club. With his name on it. "You used my money to buy the club?"

"Half of it. It was a little more complicated than that. I invested it —made it grow. And then you and I went in half on the club."

"You fucker."

"Yeah, I am. And you're an equal partner in every way. If you don't want this—us—you still collect. If you want out, you'll get half this place in cash, with interest. Your choice, Preston. Plenty of time to do whatever you want for your next chapter."

Preston blinked back tears as he stared at the lease. Jagger had planned all this, had given him a safety net to come back to.

"By the way, your name is hidden on the lease. I didn't want them to trace it back to you."

"I don't care. I want to be a part of your family."

"You always were...since that first day I saw you, pretty boy." Jagger murmured the last part affectionately, but there was also no mistaking the heat behind his words.

That heat had been there for a long time, hidden among protection and pride. Preston let that sink in for a long moment. "Speaking of family, I've got to explain to your dad."

"He told me everything so I could protect you—he wasn't worried about anything else." Jagger sighed. "Maybe I should've told you that I wanted to go totally legit. That could've made things easier."

"No, that wouldn't have. If I'm going to stand with you, it's under any circumstances. I would never ask you to give up anything."

"You didn't." Jagger smiled, brushed Preston's cheek with his knuckles. "You always made me want to be better. Whenever I was about to do something stupid, I'd think, would Preston be proud of me? Because you were off saving the world. Serving your country. All I could do was wait. Wait, and hope you'd finally come home to me. Now that you're here, I think we'll figure out the next steps together."

"You're doing all this for me?"

"Don't you get it? I'd do anything for you."

Preston put his hands on either side of Jagger's face. "Don't you get that I'd do anything for you?"

"You already have," Jagger told him. "And I'm going to make sure no one can ever fuck with you again—not because of me, at least. Not only to protect you, baby, but because I want to." Jagger's ring was sliding onto the third finger of his left hand and this was all so goddamned fast...and somehow still felt like it had taken a lifetime or more to get here. "Marry me."

Preston stared between the ring and Jagger.

"Dude, you have to answer me." Jagger looked stricken.

Preston cupped a hand to Jagger's cheek. "Do you really think I'd say no?"

"You always keep me guessing."

"I want to marry you. I love you." It came out so naturally, so easily, and Preston knew he'd never spoken truer words. Getting to this point had been hard, but they'd reached the tipping point. "I think I always have."

Jagger smiled, then grew serious. "Listen, just because you own half this place—and some other buildings in this district as well—you don't have to work with me. I get wanting to have your own thing."

"I want to do everything with you. You're the best thing that ever happened to me. Even this last year...I still knew it. I wasn't running from us. I was running from me. How I didn't understand my needs for so long."

"A lot of people don't. You had a lot of other shit to work through. You knew I'd wait."

"And you did."

"For fucking ever."

"Patience of a saint."

"Only for you, Preston. Only—and ever—for you."

AFTERWORD

Thanks again for giving this title a chance. Don't forget to keep an eye out for the other books in the Ace's Wild series. In case you missed it, Ace's Wild is a multi-author series of books that take place in the same fictional town. Each story can be read in any order. The connecting element in the Ace's Wild series is an adult store owned by Ace and Wilder. The main characters from each book will make at least one visit to Ace's Wild, where they'll buy a toy to use in their story! The only characters who cross over to each book are Ace and Wilder. And with various heat and kink levels, there's sure to be something for everyone!

NEWSLETTER SIGN-UP

Become a VIP!

Sign-up to join SE's VIP list, and receive updates about new and upcoming books, news, events and exclusive giveaways.

https://sejakes.com/newsletter/

ACKNOWLEDGMENTS

I always say that writing a book takes a village, and I'm very lucky to be surrounded by so many wonderful people who help me so much.

First, thanks to Frauke from CrocoDesigns, who does everything from websites to book formatting to covers to ads and more (and you always answers all my millions of questions so patiently!)

Thanks to Kelley York from Sleepy Fox Studio for the fantastic cover.

Thank you to Christina Lee and Riley Hart for letting me borrow Pet Land, which is featured in their Ace's Wild Series Book, SCIENCE & JOCKSTRAPS. Also, thanks to N.r. Walker for letting Jagger and Preston hang out in Evoque Nightclub—you'll see more of it in her upcoming Ace's Wild Series Book, REINDEER GAMES. And thanks to ALL the Ace's Wild Series authors mentioned at the beginning of this book, because I had a blast getting to know each and every one of you!!!

To my wonderful beta / proofer readers this time around, Melinda James Rueter and Jane Coulter, who gave all around great feedback, as usual. Your help is so appreciated, you have no idea!

To Sandra, from One Love Editing—thanks for the wonderful

edits, your always quick responses, and for being so flexible with your timing.

To Michelle Slagan from Vibrant Promotions, who put together my blog tours and so much more for this release—you made everything streamlined and simple and took so much off my plate in the process.

As always, to my readers, because you guys are really just awesome. You hang out with me on Facebook and laugh, you support me, celebrate the book releases and make everything about this job so much more fun. I'm lucky to have you all in my corner, and trust me, I know it!

Last but never least, for Zoo, Lily, Chance, and Gin—thank you for letting me escape into my fictional worlds for long periods of time and always being there for me when I return.

ALSO BY SE JAKES

MEN OF HONOR SERIES
BOUND BY HONOR

BOUND BY LAW

TIES THAT BIND

BOUND BY DANGER

BOUND FOR KEEPS

BOUND TO BREAK

* * *

PHOENIX, INC. SERIES
NO BOUNDARIES

* * *

INKED SERIES
HOLD THE LINE

THIRDS

* * *

EE LTD. UNIVERSE
FREE FALLING

* * *

HELL OR HIGH WATER SERIES
CATCH A GHOST

LONG TIME GONE

DAYLIGHT AGAIN

NOT FADE AWAY

IF I EVER

* * *

DIRTY DEEDS SERIES

DIRTY DEEDS

* * *

HAVOC MC SERIES

RUNNING WILD

RUNNING BLIND

RUNNING ON EMPTY

* * *

SINNERS

SINNERS

* * *

THE CRAVE CLUB SERIES

KEEPING CADE

SAVING SWAY

TAMING THEO (coming soon)

AXEL'S ACCORD (coming soon)

* * *

BLUEWATER BAY (Multi-Author Series)

NO EASY WAY (novella) in the *Lights, Camera, Action* Anthology

WRITING AS STEPHANIE TYLER

SALVATION

THE DEFIANCE SERIES COLLECTION

(Defiance, Redemption & Salvation)

TEMPERANCE

* * *

DIRE WOLVES SERIES

DIRE WARNING (prequel novella)

DIRE NEEDS

DIRE WANTS

DIRE DESIRES

* * *

SHADOW FORCE SERIES

LIE WITH ME

PROMISES IN THE DARK

IN THE AIR TONIGHT

NIGHT MOVES

LONELY IS THE NIGHT

* * *

HOLD SERIES

HARD TO HOLD

TOO HOT TO HOLD

HOLD ON TIGHT

HOLDING ON (novella)

* * *

HOT NIGHTS, DARK DESIRES ANTHOLOGY

NIGHT VISION (novella)

* * *

HARLEQUIN BLAZE

COMING UNDONE

RISKING IT ALL

BEYOND HIS CONTROL

ABOUT THE AUTHOR

SE Jakes is the pen name for *New York Times* bestselling author Stephanie Tyler, and half the co-writing team of Sydney Croft. First published in 2011, SE Jakes has quickly risen to be a bestselling author in the LGBT romance genre, as well as a fan favorite. Her books are frequently highlighted in *USA Today* and have been reviewed by *Library Journal* and *RT Books Magazine*. She's been nominated by several sites for Favorite M/M author and has finaled in the Goodreads M/M Romance Readers Choice Awards in 7 categories. She's a hybrid author who writes for Riptide Publishing and Samhain Publishing, and she indie publishes as well.

Visit SE Jakes at www.sejakes.com.

Stephanie Tyler is the *New York Times* bestselling author of romance novels spanning multiple genres, including Romantic Suspense, New Adult, Paranormal Romance and Contemporary Romance. She's a hybrid author who writes for multiple publishers, including Random House, NAL/Penguin, Harlequin, Carina Press, Mammoth Books, Belle Books and Samhain Publishing, as well as Riptide (as SE Jakes) and indie publishing. Her books have been translated into half a dozen languages, nominated for an RT Readers' Choice Award and garnered top picks from *RT Books Magazine* as well as starred reviews from *Publishers Weekly*. She's a frequent workshop presenter and has contributed stories for anthologies for charities, including *SEAL of My Dreams*, which has raised over 150K for the Veterans Medical Association.

Visit Stephanie Tyler at www.stephanietyler.com.

—————

Sydney Croft is the alter ego of Stephanie Tyler and Larissa Ione, two *New York Times* bestselling authors who blend their very different writing interests into adventurous tales of erotic paranormal fiction. Together, they developed a world where people with extraordinary abilities, like the power to control storms, could live and work with others like them. The series has been described as "Erotica meets the X-Men," and is unique in its own "erotic superhero romance" niche. Larissa and Stephanie live in different states and communicate almost entirely through email, though they often get together for conferences and book signings.

Visit Sydney Croft at www.sydneycroft.com.

—————

For more information:
www.stephanietyler.com
stephanie@stephanietyler.com

www.ingramcontent.com/pod-product-compliance
Lightning Source LLC
Chambersburg PA
CBHW030542130626
46552CB00006B/2375